Chapter 1

*(Author's note: This book picks up the storyline
12 months after the previous book)*

The office just wasn't the same. The furniture was the same, the decor was the same, and even the window-blinds were the same (still stuck). But without Winky, the office felt empty; it was so quiet. He might have driven me mad with all his moaning and groaning, and with all the mischief he got up to, but somehow I still missed him.

"Jill!"

The voice from the intercom almost made me jump out of my skin.

I pressed 'speak'. "Yes, Jules?"

"There's a gentleman out here. A Mr Halfway, Arnold Halfway. He wonders if you could spare him a few minutes."

"Certainly, will you show him in, please?"

"Okay, will do."

I hadn't been expecting anyone. I had no appointments booked for today. Or tomorrow. Or—well, you get the picture. So, I certainly wasn't about to turn away a prospective client.

I put him in his early sixties, maybe even older, but his hair was still thick and Jet black. As soon as he walked through the door, I noticed he had a nervous twitch in his nose—a bit like a rabbit wearing glasses. I was mesmerised.

"Miss Gooder?" the rabbit said.

"That's me." I stood up and offered my hand. "Pleased to meet you. Thank you, Jules."

"Would you like a tea or coffee, Mr Halfway?" Jules asked.

"Tea for me, please. Milk, no sugar."

"Jill?" Jules turned to me.

"I'll have tea too—with my usual sugar, please."

Jules frowned. She still couldn't get her head around my exacting sugar requirements.

"Just bring the sugar through. I'll see to it," I reassured her.

"What can I do for you, Mr Halfway?"

"Please call me Arnold; everyone does."

"Okay, Arnold. I'm Jill. How can I help?"

"I own the jewellers on Pretty Road—close to the library."

"I know the one. I bought a pair of earrings for my sister's birthday from there last year. I forget the name of the shop, though."

"Are Forever."

"Of course. Great name. So how exactly can I help you, Arnold?"

"There's been a spate of thefts recently. They've targeted several of the jewellers in Washbridge, not just my own."

"I'm sorry to hear that. I don't remember seeing anything about it in the local press."

"There was some coverage in The Bugle, but it was buried in the inside pages. They were more interested in carrying an article about a dog that had turned pink, on their front page."

"Pink?"

"I don't know the details; I didn't read the article. I'm not a big fan of The Bugle."

"Me neither." I hated that rag with a passion.

A few moments later, Jules came in, carrying a tray. This was the part I dreaded; the girl had no sense of balance whatsoever. The tea was slopping out of the cups, onto the tray. By the time she'd put it on my desk, there was as much tea on the tray as there was in the cups.

"Sorry, Jill. I seem to have spilled a bit."

"It's okay, Jules, I'll see to it. Thanks."

I kept a supply of cloths in the top drawer of my desk for just such eventualities. I wiped Arnold's cup, and put it on a coaster, then did the same with mine.

"A little bit clumsy your PA, isn't she?" He was staring at the tea on the tray.

"She's relatively new to the job, and still a little nervous."

"I see."

"You were telling me about the thefts."

"Indeed. My own shop has suffered three robberies in recent weeks."

"What about your alarm system and locks? How did the robbers get past those?"

"No, you misunderstand. The robberies didn't take place when the shop was closed; they happened during the day when it was open."

"You mean armed robberies?"

"No, thank goodness. The circumstances are very peculiar indeed. It would probably be best if I explained exactly what happened."

"Please do." If there hadn't been a break-in, and it wasn't an armed robbery, I was baffled.

"The most recent theft from my shop was exactly the same as the two previous ones. The only difference this time was that I was behind the counter. On the previous two occasions it had been one of my assistants. I was attending to a young couple who were looking for wedding rings. I had a tray of rings on the counter in front of me. Then, all of a sudden, they disappeared. All of them."

"When you say disappeared, do you mean the tray vanished?"

"No, the tray was still there, but all of the rings had gone."

"How is that possible?"

"I have absolutely no idea. That's why I'm here to see you, today. I'm hoping you might be able to throw some light on it."

"Let me get this straight. You're saying that you didn't see anyone take the rings even though the tray was right there in front of you?"

"That's precisely right. One second they were there, and the next they were gone."

"What about the young couple you were serving? Did they see anything?"

"No. They were just as baffled as I was."

"And the same thing happened on the previous two occasions?"

"Yes. The first time, it was a tray of necklaces, and the next, a tray of bracelets. But essentially, the same thing happened on each occasion."

"What do the police make of it?"

"They are completely baffled. If it wasn't for the fact that this has happened at other shops, I'm sure they would have suspected me of insurance fraud."

"Have you spoken to the other owners?"

"Yes. Although we're competitors, we all know each other quite well. They all describe exactly the same thing happening: A tray full of jewellery one moment—an empty tray the next."

"Do any of the shops have CCTV installed?"

"They all do. In a jeweller's shop, it's pretty much a necessity."

"Did the CCTV capture anything which might give a clue as to what happened?"

"Nothing at all. All the shops have a recording of the moment when the robberies took place, but none of them show anything that gives a clue as to how the jewellery disappeared."

"I've never heard of anything quite like this. And you say the police have drawn a blank?"

"Yes, pretty much. They've viewed the CCTV too. They even took the equipment away for a while to see if the recordings had been tampered with. But they've now returned it, and confirmed the recordings have not been compromised. Do you think you can help?"

"I'll be absolutely honest with you, Arnold, it's one of the more unusual cases to cross my desk, but I like a challenge, so I'll be happy to take it on."

"That's great." He stood up and offered his hand.

"I'll be in touch in a few days to arrange a visit to your shop. I'd like to talk to your staff, and view the CCTV. I'll also need a contact name at the other shops."

"That sounds fine." He gave me his business card. "Call me anytime."

After he'd left, Jules appeared, tail between her legs. "I'm sorry about the tea, Jill."

"You really have got to get to grips with the drinks

situation. Look at this tray; it's swimming in tea."

"Whenever I'm carrying a tray of drinks, I get nervous, and my whole sense of balance goes out of the window."

"From now on, it might be better if you bring them in one cup at a time."

"That's a great idea, Jill. I'll do that."

"Jules had only been back with me for a couple of months. Gordon Armitage had poached her from me not long after Winky had recruited her. Gordon had only done it to get at me—little knowing that I'd planned to let her go anyway. She'd only lasted a little over nine months at Armitage, Armitage, Armitage and Poole, but then had been unceremoniously kicked out by Gordon.

Fortunately for Jules, it was around that time that Mrs V had said that working full-time was becoming a bit of a strain, and she needed to reduce her hours to two or three days a week. I'd offered Jules the chance to job-share with Mrs V. By then, she'd gained quite a bit of experience working in reception next door. Jules had been thrilled. The money was obviously less than she'd been getting, but it was better than being out of work.

So, for the last two months, Mrs V and Jules had been job sharing. It had started off okay, but more recently, a little friction had developed between them. And, of course I had to be the referee.

Just then, I heard what sounded like a small engine.

Could it be?

I glanced out of the window. Yes! Hooray!

The microlight came sailing through the open window, and skidded across the floor, coming to a halt near the door.

"Winky! You're back! How are you?"

He took off his crash helmet and rubbed his fur. "I'm great. Have you missed me?"

"Nah. I hardly noticed you'd gone."

"Liar."

"Did you have a good time?"

"Excellent, really excellent."

Socks, Winky's brother, who'd been piloting the microlight, took off his crash helmet. "Hello there, little witchy."

I gave him an icy glare. Winky may have forgiven his brother for the way he tried to steal Bella, but that didn't mean I had to.

"Hello, Socks." I managed, through gritted teeth.

"You look really pleased to see me." He grinned.

"I trust you're not staying."

"Charming."

Winky turned to Socks. "I told you, bro, you're not welcome here. I'm glad you and I have buried the hatchet, but you can't expect Jill to forgive and forget so easily. You'd better get going. I'll keep in touch."

"Okay, bro. No worries." Socks climbed back onto the microlight, and moments later, he was flying out of the window.

"I really don't understand how you could forgive him," I said.

"I'm not one to hold grudges. Unlike you."

"I don't hold grudges."

"Are you kidding? If someone crosses you, they're on your blacklist for life. Anyway, Socks had to fork out for a new microlight. That was punishment enough. So, how are things here? Still counting paperclips and sorting rubber bands?"

"I'll have you know I've just landed a case. A jewel robbery."

"Things *are* looking up." He grabbed his backpack. "Somewhere in here I have a present."

"You shouldn't have."

"For Bella."

I should have known.

"I bought her a necklace — real gold."

"That's nice."

"Don't sulk. I've bought you something too."

"You have?"

"You didn't think I'd forget you, did you? There you go."

He handed me a small gift-wrapped package. How very sweet of him. He wasn't all bad, despite what some might say.

I ripped off the wrapping paper and opened the box.

"It's a can opener."

"An electric one."

"But, it's a can opener."

"They're much quicker than the manual ones. Which reminds me: red not pink."

Chapter 2

I'd called in at Kathy's on my way home.

"Where's Peter?"

"Working late again." She sighed.

"Is he that busy? I thought he and Jethro were able to cope with the work."

"Just lately, there's been even more work coming in. Pete's a victim of his own success—most of the new clients have come from word-of-mouth. He took on another new employee last week. I can't remember the new guy's name, but according to Pete, he's got lots of experience. Once he's up to speed, Pete should be able to cut out the late nights altogether. I hope so because I'm getting a bit cheesed off, to tell you the truth."

"The money must be nice."

"Of course it is. It's great to have a bit extra to spend on the kids. We might even manage a couple of holidays this year, and we're having a day trip to the seaside tomorrow. I just don't want it to be at the expense of Pete seeing the kids. Some days, by the time he gets home, they've already gone to bed. Anyway, enough of me, what about you? It's the *big day* tomorrow, isn't it?"

"I'd hardly call it a big day."

"You're moving into your first house together, surely that's a big day?"

"I'll be glad to get out of Jack's place, that's for sure. I'm sick of it."

"You're not sick of Jack, though?"

"Of course not. We're getting along great."

"You've got a good one there. It's not every guy who would have hung around while you dillied and dallied over making your mind up whether or not to move in with him."

"I did not dilly, nor did I dally. I gave it careful consideration for six months before I agreed."

"It looked an awful lot like dilly-dallying to me."

"That's because you moved in with Peter twenty minutes after he asked you."

"I did not. It was at least an hour." She laughed. "So what's wrong with Jack's flat, anyway?"

"I didn't realise how small it was until I was living there. The new house is much bigger."

"Will you be getting all your stuff out of storage?"

"Yes, thank goodness. I can't wait. It's been in there for three months now — ever since I sold my place. I'm hoping to throw some of his horrible furniture away."

"Has he agreed to that?"

"Not yet, but I'm working on it. If he thinks we're having those stupid bowling cups of his on display, he's got another think coming."

"You do realise that I still haven't seen this new house of yours?"

"We only signed the lease three weeks ago; the previous tenants are still in there. You can come and see it as soon as we're in, and have got it sorted."

"I still don't understand why you chose to live as far out as that."

"Because, Kathy, it was the only place we could find that we could afford. Flats are two a penny, but small houses to rent are like hen's teeth."

"Hens don't have teeth."

"Duh!"

"Oh, right. I see. A bit like rocking horse —"

"Precisely. Every time we spotted a house we liked the look of, someone beat us to it. We were lucky to get this one. Anyway, Smallwash isn't that far out of Washbridge; it's just the other side of the river Wash."

"Do you have to cross the toll bridge?"

"Don't remind me. That was the only thing that nearly put me off the house. It's not like it's a massive expansion bridge; it's a puny little thing. The river is so narrow I could practically jump across it. Jack said it was stupid to pass on the house just because of that, and I suppose he was right."

"How much is the toll?"

"Forty pence each way."

"That's hardly going to break the bank, is it?"

"It's the principle."

"What principle? The *'I'm too tight to pay forty pence'* principle?"

"Auntie Jill! Auntie Jill!" Lizzie came rushing into the room. "We're going to the seaside tomorrow."

"Lucky you. Will you be making sandcastles?"

"Yeah, and I'm going to ride on the donkeys. Why don't you come with us?"

"I can't. I'm moving into my new house, tomorrow."

"Can we come and see it?"

"Yeah, but not until we've settled in properly."

The thought of Lizzie and Mikey descending on the new house filled me with dread. The kids were all greasy fingerprints and dirty shoes. I'd just have to keep coming up with excuses to put them off.

"I'm your witness, Lizzie," Kathy said. "Auntie Jill has promised that you and Mikey can visit her as soon as they're settled in."

"Where is Mikey anyway?" I said.

"He's down at Tom Tom; it's his drum lesson today."

"Why aren't you there with him?"

"Are you kidding me? I value my sanity too much. I drop him off, and then Pete or me picks him up afterwards. Anyway, I seem to remember that you were the one who promised you'd go and listen to him."

Oh bum! Kathy's memory was way too good. She was like an elephant.

"And I will, but I've been so busy preparing for the move, and I landed a new case only today."

"What's that?"

"It's a bit of a weird one."

"Most of your cases are."

"Apparently, there have been a number of robberies from jewellers in Washbridge."

"I haven't seen anything about that on the news."

"It's had precious little coverage." I laughed. "Precious? Jewellery? Get it?"

Kathy rolled her eyes. My comedic talents were wasted here.

"The weird thing is that the jewellery just disappeared."

"What do you mean? Jewellery can't just disappear."

"It did. One minute the shop owner was showing a customer a display of jewellery, and then 'poof', the jewellery had vanished."

"Are you sure the owner hadn't been drinking?"

"It's happened to this particular shop three times, and it's happened to several other shops. It's a real mystery."

"Why did they contact you?"

"Why do you think? Because I'm Washbridge's

foremost private investigator, of course."

"And the cheapest."

"Who are you calling cheap? I'm not cheap; I'm *competitive*."

Kathy made us both a cup of tea.

"Any custard creams?" I said, more in hope than expectation.

"Yes. And no."

"What does that mean?"

"They didn't have the brand you like, so I had to buy the—err—competitive ones."

"You can't expect me to eat those cheap imitations."

"They're all I've got. Take them or leave them."

"Go on, then."

The sacrifices I had to make.

"How's Jack settling into his new job?"

"He's not over fond of the commute, but he says the people are okay, and they seem to be better organised than in Washbridge. It's not like anyone forced him to transfer over there."

"Come on, Jill. What choice did he have? How could he stay here when you and he are living together, and you get involved with at least half of the cases he's working on?"

"It's not as though I ever got in his way or caused him any problems."

"You were always stepping on his toes. He did the right thing. At least this way, he can focus on his work without having to worry that you're going to embarrass him at any moment."

"I've never embarrassed him."

"Okay, if you say so. Anyway, what about Jack's

successor here in Washbridge? Have you met him yet?"

"No. It's only a month since Jack transferred. Since then, a couple of people have stood in for him. According to Jack, his permanent replacement starts next Monday."

"What's he like, do you know?"

"Jack doesn't know anything about him apart from his name: Lee O'Reilly. Jack left him a note specifically about me—explaining who I am, and my relationship with Jack. He's asked him to cut me a bit of slack, so hopefully that will mean things are a bit easier with this new guy than they were with Jack when he first arrived. What about you? How are things at Ever?"

"Busy. Really busy. Ever since Best Wool closed down, things have been crazy. All the people who'd taken out subscriptions for Never-ending Wool are now swapping to Everlasting Wool. And, never one to miss a trick, your grandmother has offered a twenty percent discount to all those who can show that they had a subscription for Never-ending Wool."

"Miles Best was such a fool. He really had me convinced that he'd changed."

"He had everyone fooled. Even your grandmother for a while."

"Yeah, but she soon shut him down when he tried to double-cross her. He came crawling to me again, you know. He had the audacity to ask me to have another word with Grandma. I told him to sling his hook. Fool me once, shame on you. Fool me twice? I don't think so. What's happened to his shop, anyway?"

"It's all boarded up now. That's probably the last we'll see of Miles Best."

Little did Kathy know that Miles and his girlfriend,

Mindy, were still plying their trade in Candlefield. Their cake shop and tea room, Best Cakes, was located directly opposite the twins' shop, Cuppy C. For a while, he'd pretended to turn over a new leaf, and had been ultra-friendly towards Grandma, the twins and me. But it hadn't taken long for him to reveal his true colours. When he did, Grandma had easily got the better of him, and kicked him out of Washbridge. Since then, he'd turned his anger towards the twins. They'd have to be on their guard because he no doubt had more audacious plans up his sleeve.

Just then, Peter arrived home. "Hi Jill, are you here for dinner, *again*?"

"No, I can't stay. I have things to organise."

"Oh yes, it's your big day tomorrow, isn't it?"

I sighed.

"You're not allowed to call it that," Kathy said. "According to Jill, it isn't a 'big day'."

"But aren't you moving into your new house?" he said.

"Yep."

"You could try to look a little more excited about it."

"I'll be happy once we're in there. I could just do without the hassle of the move."

"You should know by now, Pete." Kathy chimed in. "Jill is allergic to anything which smacks of hard work."

"That's not true." I objected.

"What about Jack? Is he excited?" Peter said.

"Oh, yeah. He's excited enough for both of us. I'll just be relieved to get out of that poky little flat of his, and to get my furniture out of storage and into the new house."

"What about Jack's furniture?"

"What about it? If it was up to me, it would go in a skip.

Or on a bonfire. Most of it is rubbish anyway."

"Does he know that?"

"Not yet."

"Can I come and watch you tell him?" Peter grinned.

"No, you can't. Anyway, Kathy was telling me you've taken on another employee."

"Yeah, I struck really lucky. I found another guy with tons of experience who was out of work. His name is Sebastian."

No! It couldn't be. Surely not.

"He's a really good looking guy. If you weren't already with Jack, I'd put in a good word for you."

Oh boy. I deliberately hadn't told the twins that Jethro was working in Washbridge. If they found out that both he and Sebastian were here, I'd never hear the end of it.

Talking of the twins, I'd promised to go to Aunt Lucy's for dinner, so I made my excuses to Kathy and Peter. Once I was outside the house, and was sure no one was around, I magicked myself over to Candlefield.

Chapter 3

"Jill! How lovely to see you." Aunt Lucy gave me a big hug. "Isn't it your big day tomorrow?"

Apparently.

"You and Jack must be really excited about moving into the new house."

"I'll just be glad when we're in."

"I hope you'll let us come over to see the new place once you're settled."

"I suppose so. It's just difficult, you know, what with Jack not knowing that I'm a witch."

"But he does know about us, doesn't he?"

"He knows I have 'another' family. He keeps saying he'd like to meet you all."

"What's the problem, then? Why not have a housewarming party? You could invite me, Lester, Grandma, the twins and their husbands over."

Husbands? I still couldn't get my head around the idea that the twins were now married.

"It would be lovely." Aunt Lucy beamed.

"Lovely, yeah. I'll see what I can arrange."

Never. Going. To. Happen.

I know that sounds mean, but Aunt Lucy didn't realise how difficult my situation was. Let's say I did have them all over. What did I say to Jack when he asked if we could pay a return visit to them? I'd long since come to the conclusion that I needed to keep Jack and my Candlefield family apart.

"Where are Lester and the twins, Aunt Lucy?"

"Lester has to work late; he won't be able to join us for dinner, I'm afraid. But the twins should be here any minute."

"Are the guys coming with them?"

"I think so. The girls said Alan and William would be making their own way here straight from work."

"How are the twins settling into their new homes?"

"Haven't you been over to see them yet?"

"Not yet. To be fair, they have both invited me, but I've been rather busy. What about the rooms above Cuppy C? Have they managed to rent them out?"

"The girls have advertised them in The Candle, but I don't know if they've had any response yet. Are you keeping your room on there?"

"Definitely. It's handy to have a base here in Candlefield even if I don't use it very often. I suppose I should offer the twins some rent money now. I don't get the chance to help out in Cuppy C much these days."

"You could offer, but I doubt they'd take anything from you."

"Thanks again for taking Barry and Hamlet in. I didn't like to leave them above Cuppy C once the twins had moved out. I'm not sure the new tenants would have approved."

"No problem. It's doing me good to have a dog in the house; it means I get plenty of exercise."

Just then, the twins arrived. "Jill! Hi!" Amber shouted.

"Hiya, Jill!" Pearl followed her sister into the room. "It's your big day tomorrow, isn't it?"

Sheesh!

A few minutes after the twins had arrived, Alan and William turned up. William was his usual happy self. He shouted hello, and went over to join Amber. Alan, though, seemed rather subdued.

Ten minutes later, everyone was chatting when Alan tapped me on the shoulder.

"Jill, do you think I could have a quiet word in the kitchen?"

"Yeah, of course." I followed him through. "Is everything okay?"

"Two vampire friends of mine have been taken ill in the last week. One of them is still in hospital."

"I'm sorry to hear that."

"The thing is, I think someone poisoned them."

"Deliberately?"

"Yes."

"What do the police say?"

"Nothing. Everyone is trying to make out it's some kind of virus."

"What makes you think it's not."

"They're both players in my BoundBall team. I think someone is trying to nobble our team ahead of the big match."

"What match is that?"

"It's the top of the league clash. First and second place in the league play one another next. Whichever team wins is guaranteed to finish top of the league."

"If it's poison, why haven't the medical authorities notified the police?"

"I don't know. It's like there's some kind of conspiracy to cover it up. I didn't know who else to turn to. Do you have time to see if you can find out what's happening?"

"Sure. Leave it with me, and I'll see what I can dig up. Try not to worry about it."

"Easier said than done."

"I know. What does Pearl think about it?"

"She doesn't know, and I'd prefer to keep it that way. She'd only worry that I might be next."

"I understand. I won't say anything to her. Why don't you go back in there and try to enjoy dinner?"

"Okay, I'll do my best. Thanks, Jill."

While we'd been out of the room, there'd been a new arrival. Grandma was seated at the head of the table, and I could tell by the look on Aunt Lucy's face that she hadn't been expecting her.

"How much longer is dinner going to be?" Grandma grumbled.

"About five minutes, Mother. Surely even you've got enough patience to wait another five minutes."

"It had better be worth waiting for. I'm starving. What is it, anyway?"

"A nice roast chicken."

"Chicken? I had chicken the last time I was here."

"Well you've got it again. Now pour yourself a drink and be quiet."

"The way kids talk to their parents these days." Grandma tutted. "It's terrible."

Fifteen minutes later, we were all tucking into dinner; it was doubly delicious. I wish I could make gravy like Aunt Lucy. It was such a shame that Jack could never join one of these family dinners. It was becoming more and more frustrating that I wasn't able to tell him about my life in Candlefield. Whenever he asked about my birth family, I either had to change the subject, or even resort to the 'forget' spell. I hated using magic on Jack, but what choice did I have?

"Have you come to your senses yet, Jill?" Grandma said, when we'd all finished the main course, and were waiting for Aunt Lucy to serve dessert.

"Sorry?"

"I asked if you'd come to your senses yet?"

"I don't know what you're talking about, Grandma."

"I'm talking about the fact that you're still on level four when you could be on level seven."

"Do we really have to go through this all over again?"

"Mother," Aunt Lucy shouted. "I warned you about bringing this up."

"Well someone has to. The new level was introduced especially for her at the EGM, but then she refused to accept promotion to level seven."

"We're all aware of what happened," Aunt Lucy said. "It was well documented in the press at the time, and goodness knows, you bring it up at every possible opportunity."

"It bears repeating. Why would anybody refuse the opportunity to be recognised as the most powerful witch in Candlefield?"

"I've explained my reasons," I said. "A thousand times. Like I said at the EGM, I was honoured that the level six witches thought me worthy of being the first level seven witch, but *I* don't feel worthy."

"But you're the most powerful witch in Candlefield, girl. What else would it take to make you feel *worthy*?"

"I may or may not be the most powerful witch; I don't know. But that isn't the point."

"What is the point, then? Do enlighten us."

"I may have the power, but I don't yet have the experience, and I need that in order to use the power wisely."

Grandma sighed. "That same old story again?"

"It isn't a *story*, Grandma. I'd prefer to work my way through the levels like everyone else. Unless, of course, I was to win the Levels competition."

"You can't win it if you don't even enter it."

"I've explained a thousand times why I didn't enter any competitions last year. So much had happened to me in such a short period of time, that I needed a break to regroup."

"You sound like a bad corporate training video. Will you be entering the Levels competition this year, or will you still be too busy *regrouping*?"

"I will be entering it."

"And if you win, will you take the promotion to level seven?"

"No, I won't. The Levels competition should stay the same. The winner should still become a level six witch. I'll only consider moving to level seven when I'm sure I have enough experience to do justice to that position."

"You're impossible." Grandma banged her knife and fork down onto the table. "How do you think this makes me look?"

"Why should it affect you?"

"I was the one who pushed for level seven in the first place."

"Yes, but that was at the AGM. That motion was defeated, so the introduction of level seven is not down to you. Every level six witch at the latest EGM voted for the change. Except for Ma Chivers, that is."

"What good is introducing level seven, if there isn't a level seven witch?"

"There will be one eventually. Whether or not it turns out to be me is an altogether different matter."

"Who else would it be?"

"You?"

"Me?" Grandma sounded exasperated. "I have no desire to move to another level at my age. I'm perfectly happy being where I am."

"Okay, that's enough talk of the Levels." Aunt Lucy was handing out dessert. "It's time for pudding."

The toffee pudding was delicious, and thankfully seemed to take Grandma's mind off the subject of me becoming the first level seven witch. Ever since the EGM, I'd had to field questions as to why I'd turned down the opportunity. I always answered in the same way. Power alone was not enough; I needed experience too. The majority of level six witches had respected and accepted my reasoning. Unfortunately, Grandma hadn't.

After dinner, I was determined to get out of the house before Grandma got back onto her favourite hobbyhorse. I asked the twins if they wanted to come and walk Barry with me. Alan and William were busy talking sport.

"Can we go for a walk?" Barry almost knocked me over. "Jill, can we go for a walk? I love to walk. Where are we going, Jill?"

"Yes, Barry. We're going for a walk in the park."

"I love the park. Can we go now? Can we go to the park now?"

"Yes, Barry, we're going right now."

The twins walked either side of me as we made our way to the park. They both seemed very subdued.

"So, how's married life treating you two?"

"Great." Amber sighed.

"Fantastic." Pearl shrugged.

"Boy, your enthusiasm is overwhelming. Don't tell me you're fed up already. You've only been married for five minutes."

"It's not that," Amber said. "I love being married and I love being with William. I wouldn't change that for anything."

"Nor me," Pearl said. "I love being with Alan; we're really happy. And, I adore the house. There's so much more space than there was above Cuppy C."

"Yeah, I love our garden," Amber said. "And the neighbours are nice."

"So, if everything is so great, why do you both look so miserable?"

"Well—" Amber began.

"Yeah?"

"It's just—" Pearl hesitated.

"Yeah?"

"We miss one another." Amber sighed.

"Yeah, we do," Pearl agreed.

We were in the park now, so I let Barry off his lead, and then led the twins to my favourite bench.

"Let me get this straight. You miss one another?"

They both nodded.

"But when you lived together at Cuppy C, all you ever did was squabble, argue and fight. You both told me that one of the reasons you wanted to get married was to get away from each other."

"It hasn't worked out quite as well as I thought it would," Amber said.

"I know we used to argue a lot," Pearl chimed in. "But we've spent practically every day together since we were born, and now we don't see each other as often."

"Hold on. You still work together at Cuppy C, so you must see each other most days, don't you?"

"Yeah, usually five or six days a week; it depends what days we have off."

"Well then, what's the problem?"

"When we're at work, we're usually busy, and we mostly talk about work related things: the shop, the customers, and what Miles Best is up to. We don't get to talk about fun things like we used to."

"Surely there must be something you can do about that. Don't you see each other outside of work?"

They both shook their heads.

"There's your answer then. Why don't you pick one day a week to meet up outside of work, and do something together?"

"You mean the four of us?" Amber said.

"No, not with the guys. Just the two of you; like it used to be."

"I suppose we could do that, couldn't we, Pearl?" Amber said.

"Yeah. Wednesday would be best for me."

"I can't do Wednesday; it would have to be Tuesday."

"I can't do Tuesday; I go to my pottery class on Tuesday. What about Monday?"

"You know I can't do Monday. I go swimming then."

Oh, boy. It was like the good old days all over again. Time for my intervention.

"How about Friday?" I suggested.

"Yeah, Friday's okay for me," Amber said.

"Me too."

"That's settled then. Friday night is *twins night*."

"What about the guys?" Pearl said. "Do you think they'll mind?"

"If I know them, they'll be glad to get rid of you for an evening."

Chapter 4

After the twins and I had taken Barry back to Aunt Lucy's, I magicked myself back to Washbridge. I'd been living at Jack's flat for almost six months, and the place was driving me insane. When I'd agreed to move in, I hadn't really appreciated just how poky it was. And don't get me started on the furniture. I loved Jack, but the man had no taste whatsoever. A few weeks ago, we'd decided to look for a new place. We both liked the idea of a house; we'd lived in flats for too long. We couldn't afford anything very big, but we'd eventually found a small two-bed house in Smallwash, a suburb of Washbridge. Tomorrow was the day we were due to move in—tomorrow was the 'big day'.

Jack arrived home ten minutes after me.

"How was work?" I said.

"Okay. A bit busy, but I'm starting to find my way around now. What about you? Have you met my successor yet? He should have started by now."

"Lee O'Riley? No, not yet. The one consolation is that he can't be any worse than you were when you first arrived here."

"Thanks, petal. I'll take that as a compliment."

I gave him a look. He knew I hated it when he called me that.

"It's a term of endearment." He put on that innocent face of his.

"If you call me that one more time, you'll get my foot up your backside. Let's see how endearing you find that."

"You're touchy. Had a bad day?"

"No. Quite good, actually. I've landed a new client."

"Anything juicy?"

"It's certainly intriguing. A jewel robbery."

"Was it a break-in?"

"No, the thefts took place while the shops were open, but no one saw the robbers."

"What do you mean, no one saw them?"

"There have been several robberies, and they all follow the same pattern. One minute there's a tray of jewellery on the counter, the next minute the jewellery has gone. Poof!"

"That's impossible."

"You'd think so, but that seems to be what happened. It's on CCTV."

"Are the police involved?"

"I assume so, but according to the guy who came to see me today, nothing much has happened. Typical police."

"Hey! Watch it." He grinned. "So what have you found out so far?"

"Give me a chance. I only took on the case today, and I won't get the opportunity to do anything tomorrow, will I?"

"You were the one who wanted to move house."

"I seem to recall it was a joint decision."

"You telling me *we move or else*, doesn't constitute a joint decision. I like this place."

"Well you'd better say your goodbyes because after tomorrow, this poky little hole will belong to someone else."

***

The next morning, Jack's phone rang at stupid o'clock.

Still half asleep, I went into the kitchen to make coffee while he took the call in the bedroom.

"I've got to go into work." He yawned.

"What do you mean, *you've got to go in*? Have you forgotten we're moving today?"

"I know, but there was a double homicide last night. Everyone has to go in; all leave has been cancelled."

"You can't be serious!"

"There's nothing I can do."

"I can't manage the move by myself. I thought the plan was that I'd go to the new house, and you'd stay here until they'd collected everything?"

"It was, and it can still work. Everything here is packed and ready. I'll drop in at the removals company, and give them a key to this place. They don't need anyone to be here—they know what needs to be collected because we've put stickers on everything. The storage people will bring all of your stuff. You just need to be at the new place to supervise when both of them arrive."

"Where am I going to put everything in the new house?"

"Put it where you can. We'll sort it out when I get back tonight."

"Can't you call in sick?"

He gave me that look of his. "I have to get going. I'll see you at the house, tonight. Okay?"

"Yeah, great. Thanks very much!"

Fantastic! It looked like it was all on me. I'd thought I was going to have an easy day. I'd planned to put my feet up while Jack organised everything. I couldn't even call Kathy to ask if Peter could give me a hand because she,

Peter and the kids were having a day trip to the seaside.

Unless—maybe if they hadn't set off, I could still catch them.

What? Sheesh, I was only joking. Even I wouldn't be so horrible as to spoil the kids' day at the seaside.

After breakfast, I drove to the new house. We'd been there several times since we first viewed it, but this was the first time I'd travelled there by myself. When I was about half a mile from the toll bridge, I came across a queue of standing traffic. Great! This day was getting better and better. We'd never encountered any traffic jams on our previous visits. In fact, we'd both remarked on how quiet the roads were.

Some of the people ahead of me were beeping their horns. I'm not sure what good they thought that was going to do. After not moving for over five minutes, I turned off the engine, and walked down the line of cars.

"What's going on?" I asked a man walking in the opposite direction.

"There's a new guy taking the fees on the toll bridge. He doesn't have a clue what he's doing. I've been working the night shift. At this rate, by the time I get home, I'll have to turn straight around and go back to work again."

Back in the car, I switched the radio on. It looked as though it was going to be a long wait.

It was another twenty minutes before I eventually reached the bridge. There was only one man on duty in the small booth; he was collecting the fees by hand. Why didn't they have automated machines?

"Forty pence, please," the man said. It was a voice I recognised. A voice I hadn't heard for over six months. A voice I thought I left behind when I moved into Jack's place.

"Mr Ivers?"

"Hello, Jill." He looked as surprised as I did. "I wondered where you'd gone. You just disappeared overnight."

Behind me, people were shouting, and beeping their horns.

"I moved in with Jack. You remember him, don't you? The policeman."

"You didn't leave a forwarding address. I haven't been able to get your newsletter to you."

"Oh yeah, sorry about that. I must have forgotten." Snigger.

"Not to worry. I knew you'd want them, so I saved all the back issues. There are twenty-four now. If you let me have your new address, I'll bring them over to you."

"Actually, we're moving into our new house in Smallwash, today. I don't remember the address." I lied.

"In that case, I'll bring your back issues to work with me. The next time you come over the bridge, you can collect them, and pay me."

Beep, beep, beep.

The people in the queue behind me were getting angrier and angrier.

"I suppose I'd better get going, Mr Ivers. How much is the toll, again?"

"Forty pence, please."

"There you go." I gave him the correct change.

"Thanks. It's nice to see you again, Jill."

"And you, Mr Ivers."

"And don't worry, I won't forget your newsletters."

Surely this day couldn't get any worse.

I parked on the road because I wanted to leave the driveway clear for the removal van. I was such a numbskull; why hadn't I thought to bring something to eat and drink with me? Just a few custard creams and tea or coffee would have done.

The removal van was supposed to arrive at any moment, but it was likely to be much later if it was held up by Mr Ivers. Just then, there was a knock at the door — perhaps they'd lost patience, and rammed the barrier on the toll bridge. I glanced out of the front window, but there was no sign of a removal van. Whoever was at the door knocked again.

"Hi." It was a woman, probably in her late fifties. She had a huge smile, and was holding a plate.

"Welcome, neighbour. I live next door." She gestured to the house behind her. "My name is Rita. Rita Rollo."

"Nice to meet you, Mrs Rollo. I'm Jill Gooder." I offered my hand, but then realised that her hands were full of plate.

"Will you be living here alone, Jill?"

"No. Jack's had to work. He'll be here later tonight."

"I made this for you." She glanced down at the plate.

"That's very sweet of you. It's a pity you dropped it, but it's the thought that counts."

"Dropped it?" She looked puzzled.

I glanced again at the monstrosity on the plate.

"Dropped? I meant — err — topped. It's a pity you topped it because I really like un-topped cake."

Now, she looked even more confused.

"I call it Chocolate Surprise." She handed me the 'cake'.

"Thanks. It's very — err — chocolaty. And definitely

surprising."

"I love to bake. It's my only hobby."

"Have you been doing it long?"

"Oh yes. Years and years. In fact, I enter all the local W.I. competitions."

"Have you won any?"

"Not yet, but I did come third in the fruit cake section last time out."

"That's good. Were there many entrants?"

"Not many. Three, I think. Do you bake, Jill?"

"Me? No, I can't bake for toffee."

"Maybe I could give you lessons some time."

"Yeah, maybe. Although I am very busy."

Just then, I spotted the removal van coming up the road.

"This looks like our stuff. I'll have to go. Thanks again for the — err — cake."

I put the plate onto the breakfast bar, and hurried back to the front door.

"Morning, love," a man with a flat cap greeted me. "I don't know why you're moving here. That bridge is a nightmare."

"It's not always as bad as that. There's a new man working there today."

"My pet ferret could take cash faster than that muppet. Where do you want us to put your stuff, love?"

It was the furniture from Jack's flat.

"Would you take it upstairs and put it in the back bedroom?"

"All of it? Will there be room?"

"Just pile it in there as best you can."

"Okay, if you're sure."

It took them a little under an hour to get everything

upstairs. The back bedroom was absolutely jam packed. I could barely open the door, but at least it had hidden away all that hideous furniture.

My own stuff was coming from the storage depot. Annoyingly, they hadn't been able to give me a precise time when they would arrive. By mid-morning, I was really peckish, and would have killed for a custard cream. There was a corner shop only a five-minute walk away. If I hurried, I could pick up some custard creams and a drink, and be back in no time. To be on the safe side, I put a note on the door: *'Back in five minutes'*.

Chapter 5

The corner shop was imaginatively named 'Corner Shop'. Even though it was very small, it carried an enormous range of stock. There was very little room between the aisles of shelves. The man behind the counter was unremarkable except for his toupee. He was reading a newspaper, which he'd laid out on the counter. Every time he leaned forward, the toupee slid forward too. On one occasion, it actually dropped onto the counter in front of him. This didn't seem to faze him though; he simply picked it up and popped it back onto his head. It was really quite hilarious.

"Hi," I said.

"Hello there. I haven't seen you in here before. Are you new to the area?"

"We're moving in just up the road. I was hoping I might be able to pick up some custard creams. Do you have any?"

"The king of biscuits? Of course."

I liked this man already.

"My name is Jugg, but everyone calls me Toby."

"That's very good." I laughed.

He seemed puzzled. "Toby's my first name."

"Right. Of course. Well, Toby, perhaps you could point me in the direction of the custard creams."

"I can do better than that. I'll take you to them." He walked around the counter and led the way down the aisle. "Here they are."

As he stooped down to pick up a packet, his toupee slipped off his head, and landed on the floor. I didn't know where to look, so pretended to check my phone.

Toby didn't miss a beat. He simply picked it up, and slapped it back on his head.

"These are on a one for two offer."

"Don't you mean a two for one offer?"

"Oh yes, of course. I always get that mixed up."

"BOGOF."

"There's no need for that." He looked horrified.

"No, I didn't mean *bog off*. I meant B-O-G-O-F. Buy One Get One Free."

"BOGOF? How very clever. Did you just come up with that? You should be in retail. I must start to use it. It's quite brilliant."

"How much are the custard creams?"

"Have those on me. Call it a 'welcome to the neighbourhood' gift, and also by way of a thank you for such a brilliant idea. I'm going to make some BOGOF signs right now."

A free packet of custard creams? Things were beginning to look up.

Spoke too soon.

When I got back to the house, the front garden was piled high with storage boxes and furniture. My furniture! There was no sign of the storage company's van.

Mrs Rollo came charging over.

"I told them you'd only gone to the shop. I pointed out the note you left on the door, but they weren't interested. They said they didn't have time to hang around, and just dropped it all on the garden. What on earth will you do?"

"I don't know, but thank you for trying to stop them."

"Not at all, dear. Some people just don't care. I'd help you myself, but I'm afraid my back isn't up to it."

"I understand. Thanks anyway."

There was no way I was going to be able to carry all that furniture inside by myself. After checking all around to make sure no one was watching, I cast a spell to shrink all the boxes and furniture. They were now small enough to fit inside a doll's house. I quickly scooped them up, and carried them inside. Once I'd put everything in the correct room, I reversed the spell. Easy peasy!

There was a knock at the door. If the storage men had come back, they were going to get a piece of my mind.

"Mrs Rollo? Is everything all right?"

"No. Something terrible has happened. Someone has stolen your furniture! One minute it was in the garden, and the next—" She stopped dead because she'd just spotted the furniture in the living room. "It's in here?"

"Yes, I managed to get it all inside."

"However did you do that so quickly?"

That was a very good question.

"I do a lot of physical work in my job, so it wasn't difficult."

"Oh? Right." She still looked puzzled. "All's well that ends well, I suppose. I'd better be going. Bye, then."

Oh bum! I'd only just moved in, and I'd already given the neighbour reason to be suspicious of me. I'd have to be much more careful with my use of magic from now on.

Jack eventually turned up just after nine o'clock that evening.

"It's been a long day. I'm shattered." He glanced around. "Where's all my stuff?"

"Have you eaten?" I tried to change the subject.

He checked the living room and dining room, and then

made his way upstairs to the main bedroom. I followed.

"None of my stuff is here. Didn't they deliver it?"

"Yes, it arrived okay."

He followed my gaze as I glanced at the spare bedroom. As he opened the door, a chair almost fell on top of him.

"What's it all doing in here?"

"I thought it was only fair. I've lived in your flat for the last six months, and had to put up with your stuff."

"What do you mean *put up with it*? Couldn't we have a mix? It doesn't have to be one or the other. I've got some really good stuff in here."

"Where?"

"These chairs for example."

They were beyond hideous.

"You left me in the lurch today, so I had to do the best I could. My furniture was already set out by the time your stuff arrived," I lied. "I thought it would be easier to put yours in here, and get things out as and when we need them." Like never.

He looked far from convinced. "Okay. I guess so."

We made our way back downstairs, and into the kitchen.

"What on earth is that?"

"That's a 'welcome' present from our next door neighbour, Mrs Rollo."

"Yes, but *what* is it?"

"A cake."

"You really should be more careful, Jill. After all the work she'd put into baking it, you go and drop it."

***

When I arrived at the office the next morning, Mrs V

was chuntering away about something.

"Are you okay, Mrs V?"

"I'm fine. It's the *others* that are the problem. How did your house move go?"

"Jack had to work, so it was left to muggins here to sort everything out."

"Oh dear. I bet that was a disaster, then."

"Thanks for the vote of confidence."

"Organisation isn't exactly your strong suit, is it, Jill? That's why you have me."

"It actually went okay. We got all of my furniture out of storage. It looks great in the new house."

"What about Jack's stuff?"

"I put it all in the back bedroom."

"How does he feel about that?"

"He'll come around to the idea." Eventually.

"Anyway Jill, you and I need to have words."

Oh dear. That didn't sound good.

"I am rather busy this morning, Mrs V."

"That will have to wait. This is important. It's about Jules."

I had a feeling it might be. "What about her?"

"That young *lady* shows no respect for me at all."

"You never see one another. Jules works different days to you."

"I mean in the way she treats my possessions. Look, I'll show you."

She beckoned me around the desk, and pointed to the bottom left-hand drawer. "This is my knitting drawer. And this." She opened the bottom right-hand drawer. "This is my crochet drawer. Does that look like crochet to you?"

The only thing in the drawer was a pile of magazines. "Don't tell me Jules has thrown your crochet out."

"Good heavens, no. I wouldn't be sitting here talking to you now if she had. I'd be hunting her down."

"So where is your crochet?"

"Here!" She opened the bottom left-hand drawer.

"I thought you said that was your knitting drawer?"

"It is, but if you look closely, you'll see my knitting drawer now contains knitting *and* crochet."

"So, let me get this straight. Jules has moved your crochet out of that drawer, and put it into this one."

"Correct."

"Is that so terrible?"

"That's not all she's done." Mrs V glared at me. "Look! This is where I keep my patterns."

This time she was pointing to the middle right-hand drawer.

"Does that look like patterns to you?"

"No, it looks like makeup."

"Correct."

"It looks to me like Jules has taken the drawers on the right hand side of the desk, and left you with the drawers on the left."

"Precisely."

"But surely, now you're sharing jobs, that's only fair. Isn't it?"

"I might have known you'd side with her. How long have I worked for you, and your father before you?"

"A long time."

"I think that entitles me to keep my wool, crochet and patterns in the drawer of my choice. Don't you, Jill?"

"Well—err—it—" I glanced at my office door. "Was that

my phone?"

"I didn't hear anything."

"I think it was. We'll talk about this later."

I took that opportunity to slip through to my office. I'd needed that little outburst like I needed a hole in the head. At least I'd have some sanctuary in my own office.

"Jill! This is an emergency," Winky yelled.

Once again, I'd spoken too soon.

"What's wrong? Have you run out of salmon?"

"Nothing so trivial. Bella is leaving."

"What do you mean *leaving*?"

"Leaving! As in going away. No longer here."

"I know what the word means, but why? She hasn't run away with Socks again, has she?"

Winky gave me his one-eyed death-stare. "No, she has *not* run off with Socks or anyone else for that matter. Bella and I are an item now. The humans she lives with have decided they're going to live somewhere else."

"When did all of this happen?"

"I've only just found out. Bella sent me a message via helicopter."

"How is she taking it?"

"How do you think? She's devastated."

"I'm really sorry, but I'm not sure what I can do about it."

"You'd better think of something, and quick, because if I lose Bella, I'm going to be terminally depressed. Do you really want to have to live with that?"

I didn't. It was bad enough living with a happy Winky. Living with a depressed Winky didn't bear thinking about.

"Okay, I'll see what I can do. But I'm not promising

anything."

"If Bella leaves me, I don't know what I'll do. I'll probably sink into the depths of despair." He put a paw to his head.

"Okay, enough of the amateur dramatics. I get it."

Chapter 6

By the time Mrs V brought in my mid-morning cuppa, she seemed a little brighter.

"How's Armi, Mrs V?"

"He's very well, thanks. We had a lovely weekend. We went to the Washbridge carnival on Saturday. Armi won a coconut."

"That's great. Has Armitage, Armitage, Armitage, and Poole moving out of here had much of an impact on your relationship?"

"Of course—it was inevitable. When Armi worked next door he could pop in during the day, or I could go around there. It was only for a few minutes—perhaps a cup of tea or a chat, but we both enjoyed it. Since they moved across town, I only get to see him at weekends or occasionally in the evening."

"How's he taking it?"

"He didn't want to move, but he didn't have a say in it. It was Gordon who was calling the shots, as always. Once Gordon realised he was never going to get you out, he decided to cut his losses, and find new offices. The only good thing that came out of it is that we don't have to put up with that awful Gordon Armitage. I certainly don't miss him."

"Me neither."

"Have you heard anything from the landlord about who our new neighbours are likely to be, Jill?"

"No. I've spoken to Zac a couple of times. He said there were a few interested parties, but there's nothing concrete yet. It could be empty for some time, I guess. But, let's be honest, whoever we get can't be any worse than Gordon

Armitage."

"That's true."

I'd just taken a sip of my tea when Kathy walked into the office.

"How come you always turn up when I've got the custard creams out?"

"Is there a time when you *don't* have them out?"

"I suppose you want one?"

"Two actually." She grabbed them before I could snatch the packet away. "A cup of tea would be nice, too."

"Mrs V!" I shouted. "Would you make Kathy a cup of tea, please?"

"How's the job-sharing going between Mrs V and the new girl?" Kathy asked.

"Her name is Jules, and it's not going great. There's a certain amount of friction."

Mrs V brought Kathy's tea through. "There you go. It's nice to make tea for someone who has uncomplicated sugar requirements."

"Thank you, Mrs V." Kathy smiled. "How's the knitting going?"

"It would be going a lot better if I could find my patterns. My desk isn't my own anymore."

"I see what you mean," Kathy said, after Mrs V had gone back to the outer office. "Sounds like a storm in a teabag."

"Cup."

"What?"

"It's a storm in a tea*cup* not a storm in a tea*bag*."

"Why do you always have to be so pedantic, Jill? So what has Jules done to upset Mrs V, exactly?"

"She's commandeered some of the drawers in Mrs V's desk. Mrs V is none too impressed, but it'll all come out in the wash."

Kathy took a slurp of tea — and I do mean a slurp. Gross!

"I must say, Jill. I never thought you'd get around to doing it."

"Doing what? Getting my own house?"

"No. Getting a new sign for this place."

"Do you like it?"

"I'm not mad on the colours, but at least it has *your* name on it."

"What's wrong with the colours?"

"White text on orange? It doesn't really say private investigator to me. More tanning salon."

"You never did have an eye for colour."

"If you say so. Has anyone moved in next door yet?"

"Not yet, but I don't imagine it'll stay empty for long. This part of Washbridge is still very popular."

"Anyway, the *real* reason I popped over is, I've got two bits of news to tell you."

"Good or bad?" I already knew the answer; Kathy was grinning from ear to ear.

"Good news. Definitely good news. Which would you like first, the good news or the gooder news?" Kathy laughed at her own joke.

"Hey, this is *my* office. I do the comedy routines in here."

"Can't say I'd noticed."

"Cheek! Go on, what's the good news?"

"I've got four tickets for the hottest show in town."

"Four? So, that's one for you, one for Peter, one for Lizzie and one for Mikey?"

"No, it's not a kids' thing. The tickets are for me, Pete, you and Jack."

"Tickets for what?"

"I've already told you; it's the hottest show in Washbridge. These tickets are like gold dust."

"According to you. What is it?"

"You'll thank me when I tell you."

"If you ever get around to it."

"You know Ultimate Factor, right?"

"Is that that awful talent contest on TV?"

"There's nothing awful about it. It's the top rated program across all the networks."

"It's still rubbish."

"How would you know? Have you ever watched it?"

"I don't need to watch it to know it's rubbish. It's a talent contest. All the acts in talent contests are rubbish."

Oh bum. What had I just said?

"Have you forgotten that Lizzie regularly enters talent contests? Are you saying she's rubbish?"

"No, no. Of course not. That's different, obviously. I just meant TV talent contests. Anyway, what's this got to do with the tickets you've bought?"

"They're for Ultimate Factor Live. The top acts from the previous year's show go out on tour, and they're coming to the Washbridge Arena."

"Washbridge Arena?" I laughed. "Don't you mean the Astoria?"

"They've renamed it. It's now the Washbridge Arena."

"It's not even an arena. It's just a poky old theatre."

"Well, anyway, Ultimate Factor Live is coming there, and I have four tickets."

"I don't want to go, and Jack certainly won't."

"That's where you're wrong. He's totally up for it."

"Please tell me you didn't go to Jack behind my back."

"I knew if I asked you first, you'd say 'no'."

"So, you *did* go behind my back?"

"See, when you say it like that, it sounds bad. Did you know that Jack is a big fan of Ultimate Factor?"

"He watches all kinds of rubbish on TV. I usually go into the other room to listen to music. Classical, obviously."

"Which composer?"

Oh bum! Quick, think of a composer! "Bach."

"Bach, eh? What in particular?"

"I like all his stuff."

"Stuff? I'm not sure Bach wrote *stuff*."

"Anyway, when is this show?"

"In a couple of weeks."

"Great. Can't wait."

"You do know who won last year's Ultimate Factor, don't you?"

"How would *I* know. Was it a performing gerbil?"

"Now you're just being stupid. You *should* know — you could have been one of them."

"What are you talking about?"

"Do you remember Lizzie's first talent contest?"

How could I forget? "Yeah?"

"We saw them perform there — The Coven."

"You mean those three women in the sparkly leotards?"

"That's them. Didn't you say they'd asked you to join them?"

"Yeah, they did."

"Looks like you missed a golden opportunity there. If you'd joined them, you'd be a superstar now. They must be making a packet what with the tour and the TV appearances."

"Are you sure we're talking about the same people?"

"Yeah, they won by a landslide of votes."

"How?"

"People love them. They especially like the bit at the end of their routine where they get down on one knee, then jump up and say —"

"We. Are. The Coven."

"Yeah. That goes down a bomb."

"They wanted me to be the 'The'. If I'd agreed to join them —"

"You would have been rich and famous now."

"Well, that's depressing. And that was your *good* news, apparently. What's your *gooder* news?"

"First, you must promise you won't say a word to your grandmother."

"What have you done now? Have you broken something in the shop?"

"No, I haven't done anything wrong. I've been offered a job."

"In another wool shop?"

"No. At Wool TV."

"Doing what? Making the tea?"

"Cheek. No. Somebody saw me on the reality show they filmed in Ever. When one of their presenters left recently, he suggested me as his replacement. They called, and asked me to go in for a chat, but it sounds like the job is as good as mine."

I was lost for words. My sister was about to become a TV presenter, and *I'd* thrown away the opportunity to be a rich superstar. Things kept on getting better and better.

I'd promised Alan that I'd investigate what he was convinced was the poisoning of his two friends. He'd given me their names and contact details. One of them was still in hospital.

It was the first time I'd visited the Candlefield Hospital—it was an impressive building located a couple of miles from the centre of town. I started at the reception desk.

"Could you tell me where I can find David Warren?"

"Warren, you say? Is that W-A-R-R-E-N?"

"Yes, that's him."

"And you are?"

"I'm his sister, Isabelle Warren."

The woman, a young werewolf, checked her computer screen.

"Oh yes. He was brought in a few days ago. He's on Cosmo ward; that's on the third floor."

"Will I be able to see him now?"

"Yes. Visiting times are anytime between ten am and seven pm."

As I was supposed to be this guy's sister, I could hardly ask one of the nurses which one of the patients was David Warren. Instead, I walked down the ward, glancing left and right at the notes that were attached to the end of each bed.

When I was halfway down the ward, I spotted his name. The vampire was probably in his early twenties, but looked much older.

"David! David! Are you awake?"

He opened one eye. "Who are you?"

"Alan sent me. My name is Jill Gooder, I'm a private investigator. I'm cousin to Amber and Pearl, the twins."

"I know them." He pulled himself into a sitting position. "They own the cake shop."

"That's right. I wondered if I could ask you a few questions?"

"I'll try, but I'm not feeling too great."

"That's really what I wanted to talk to you about. According to Alan, you're the second member of his BoundBall team to have been affected."

"Really? I didn't know. Who's the other one?"

"Bobby."

He nodded. "Poor old Bobby. Is he in here too?"

"No, I believe they've let him go home. Can you tell me how this all started?"

"I was perfectly well; in fact, I'd been playing BoundBall. Then, I started to feel weak and a teeny bit dizzy. The next thing I knew I woke up in here. I must've collapsed."

"Had you eaten anything unusual?"

"No, but then I'm a bit of a fussy eater, so I tend to stick to the same diet all the time."

"The doctors are saying it's a virus."

"That's what they told me too, but I don't buy it. I reckon it was the blood."

"Blood?"

"The synthetic blood. All the vampires in Candlefield drink it. No human blood allowed."

"Of course. What makes you think it might be that?"

"I'd had a new batch delivered that day, and it was not long after I had my first drink that I began to feel off it."

"Delivered? You don't get it from a shop, then?"

"No. All synthetic blood is delivered to the door."

"Did it look or — err — taste — any different?"

"No. It was the same as always."

"Okay. Thanks, David. I'll let you get back to sleep. I hope you feel better soon."

***

I'd only been back at the office for a few minutes when Mrs V popped her head around my door.

"There's a detective to see you. He says he's taken over from Jack Maxwell."

"Ah, right. Send him straight in, would you, please?"

So, Lee O'Reilly had decided to pay me a visit. That was promising. Perhaps Jack's note had convinced him that we could work harmoniously together.

Mrs V showed him through, and asked if he'd like a drink.

"Not for me, thank you." His accent took me a little by surprise. It sounded like he hailed from the midlands.

"Mr O'Reilly." I flashed a welcoming smile. "Do have a seat."

He sat down, but didn't return my smile. "That's not my name."

"Oh, sorry. I thought you were Lee O'Reilly."

"I *am* Leo Riley."

"I thought you just said you weren't Mr O'Reilly?"

"I'm not Mr O'Reilly. I'm Leo Riley."

I was totally confused, and it must have shown.

"My first name is Leo; my last name is Riley. Leo Riley."

"Ah, I see. Leo Riley, not Lee O'Reilly." We weren't

getting off to the best of starts. "Sorry for the confusion. I thought—never mind. Do I call you Leo?"

"You can call me Detective Riley."

"Right, okay. Welcome to Washbridge, Detective Riley. How are you settling in?"

"It's too early to say, but as I was passing by, I thought I should pop in. It seems my predecessor, Jack Maxley—"

"Maxwell."

"Whatever. He left me some sort of cryptic note about you and your business."

"Jack and I are actually in a relationship."

"I'm not interested in any of that, but I got the distinct impression from the note that he thought I should treat you with kid gloves."

"I'm sure that's not what he intended."

"Regardless, I want to make it perfectly clear that I'm a great believer that the police should be the ones to enforce the law and solve crimes. We don't need, and certainly don't want, any interference from *amateurs*."

"I'm sorry you feel that way. If you check your records, you'll find that I've actually helped to solve several cases—some of them quite high profile ones."

"I'm really not interested in anything which may have happened in the past. I'm only interested in the here and now. I want to make it absolutely clear that I will not tolerate you or any other amateur sleuth interfering in police business. Got it?"

"Oh yeah. I've got it." The asshat has spoken.

"Good. I'm glad we understand one another." He stood up. "Thank you for your time."

With that, he left.

It was like déjà vu, and put me in mind of my early

encounters with Jack. It seemed I would be butting horns with the police once again.

Fantastic!

Winky jumped onto my desk. "Making friends and influencing people again, I see."

"Shut it! I'm not in the mood."

"Have you figured anything out, yet?"

"About what?"

"About Bella, of course."

"Not yet, but I'm on it."

He one-eyed me suspiciously. "You'd forgotten all about it, hadn't you?"

"Of course not. It's my very top priority, but I did move house this weekend. That takes a lot of work."

"Eureka!" he shouted. "That's it!"

"What's it?"

"The perfect solution!"

"Will you stop talking in riddles?"

"Me and Bella can move into your new house."

Oh bum!

"That's not possible."

"Why not?"

"We're only renting, and the lease won't allow it."

"Why didn't you choose somewhere that would allow pets?"

"I tried, honestly, but there are so few properties available. It was this or nothing."

"Bella is moving out next week, so you'd better get your backside in gear."

"I will. I promise."

"You better had. If Bella leaves, I'm going to be

unbearable."

Would I even notice the difference?

Chapter 7

Arnold Halfway had provided me with a list of the other jewellers' shops that had suffered the same fate as his own. The nearest to my office was one called 'All That Glitters', which was a few doors down from Tom Tom. I'd called ahead and been told to ask for the manager — a Mr Poster.

"You must be Jill."

"That's right. Mr Poster?"

"Everyone calls me Bill. Would you like to come through to the back? We can talk better in there." He led the way behind the counter and into a small office.

"Tell me, Bill, how many robberies have you had?"

"Just the one. I know that Are Forever has had three. That's awful."

"Would you describe exactly what happened?"

"I will, but this is probably going to sound crazy."

"Don't worry about that. Just tell me everything you remember."

"Okay. I was actually in the shop at the time, but I wasn't serving anyone. My assistant, Ms Jameson, was attending to a young lady who was looking at some rather expensive bracelets. Ms Jameson had the tray of bracelets on the counter, so the young lady could get a closer look at them. Then, all of a sudden, the tray was empty. Just like that. One minute they were there, the next they'd gone."

"And you saw this happen?"

"Yes. Ms Jameson is a new employee. I was watching to make sure she was handling the sale according to our procedures."

"It's very difficult to understand how the bracelets could have just disappeared like that."

"I know, and if I hadn't seen it with my own eyes, I would never have believed it either. But that's exactly what happened. We have CCTV coverage if you'd like to take a look."

"Yes, please. That would be very helpful."

A few minutes later, we were seated in front of the computer. Bill Poster soon located the correct recording.

"That's Ms Jameson. And that's the young lady she was serving. You can clearly see the bracelets in the tray on the desk."

He was right. The recording quality was very good. The tray was obviously full of bracelets.

"Keep watching," he said. "Any moment now."

I stared at the screen in the hope that I'd spot something everyone else had missed. But then, suddenly, the tray was empty. I'd seen nothing. No one had come into the shop; no one had approached the counter. And yet, the tray had been emptied of its contents.

What was going on?

***

Alan's other friend, who had also been taken ill, was Bobby. From what Alan had told me, the hospital had once again put the illness down to a virus. Bobby lived at home with his parents, even though he was about the same age as Alan. It was his mother who greeted me at the door.

"You must be Jill Gooder; I've heard so much about you. It's awfully good of you to do this for us."

"I'm glad to help. Is it okay to speak to your son?"

"Of course. Bobby's been expecting you. He's still quite poorly, but much better than he was. For a while there, we were worried we might lose him."

"So I understand."

"He's in here, I'll leave you two alone."

Bobby was sitting up in bed. He looked very pale, but his eyes were bright.

"Hi there, I'm Jill."

"Have a seat. Thanks for coming."

"Look, I'll get straight to the point. The medical profession and the police are saying this is some kind of forty-eight-hour virus. Alan and David think otherwise. What about you?"

"I'm convinced I was poisoned, and no one will persuade me otherwise."

"Tell me what happened."

"I'd just taken delivery of a new supply of synthetic blood. I had my first drink in the morning, and in the afternoon, I started to feel really ill. The next thing I knew, I woke up in hospital."

"Do you still have the bottle you drank from?"

"No. According to my mother, the police took away the complete supply."

"Did they get back to you to tell you what their tests showed?"

"No. My mother had to call them. They said the tests didn't show anything unusual."

"But you don't believe them?"

"Not for a minute. I think they just wanted to dispose of the evidence. My mother says I should let it drop, but I can't. This could happen to someone else, and they might not be as lucky as I was."

By the time I left, Bobby was starting to flag. The more I learned about this, the more I was beginning to buy into the cover-up theory. But why would the authorities be so keen to bury this story? Who were they trying to protect?

***

It would have been more than my life was worth to go back to the office without at least trying to find out what was happening with Bella. I dropped into the building across the road from my office, and made my way to Bonnie and Clive's apartment.

"Hello, Jill." Bonnie had never answered the door to me before.

"Hi. Is Clive in?"

"He's in bed, I'm afraid. He hasn't been well for quite some time."

"Oh dear. I'm sorry to hear that."

"He's going to be okay, but it was touch and go for a while. It's going to be a long process. We'll be moving soon to more suitable accommodation."

"So I heard."

"Really? Who from?"

Oh bum!

"From—err—I—err—I don't actually remember who told me. Where are you going?"

"To Lakeminster."

"That's quite a long way away, isn't it?"

"Yes, but it's close to our daughter. It's a retirement community with bungalows. There are no stairs for Clive to have to deal with. It will be much better for him."

"That makes sense. When will you be moving?"

"Next week, actually. Our problem now is what to do with Bella."

"Aren't you taking her with you?"

"We'd love to. She means the world to us, but they don't allow pets. We nearly didn't agree to go for that very reason, but our daughter insisted, and she's probably right."

"What will happen to Bella?"

"I don't know. We're desperately trying to find someone to take her. Actually, we should have thought of this before. Would you take her, Jill?"

"Me? I'm sorry, but I can't. I'm not meant to have any pets in the office. I can just about get away with the one."

"That's a pity, because you're obviously a cat person. We want her to go to someone who loves cats. Do you know of anyone who could offer her a home? Preferably someone who lives in this area."

"Not offhand, Bonnie, but I'll certainly give it some thought. If I come up with anything, I'll pop back to see you, or give you a call."

"Thanks. We'd be so grateful."

"Give my best wishes to Clive."

What was I supposed to do now? If Winky found out that they'd offered Bella to me, but I'd said no, he would probably kill me. I had to find someone who would take Bella in. But, who?

***

To my amazement, Jack was already home when I got in. I could smell something cooking as soon as I walked through the door.

"Jill!" he shouted from the kitchen. "I'm in here."

"Wow, what's all this? How come you're home?"

"I got finished on a case early, and couldn't see any point in picking up the next one so late in the day. And besides, I've worked a few lates recently, so they owe me a few hours. I thought I'd come home and make dinner for us."

"I'm liking that idea."

"Don't get used to it. I don't know how often I'll be able to get away early."

"It smells good. What is it?"

"I've made a beef casserole. I hope that's okay."

"Yeah, lovely."

And it *was* lovely. I had to hand it to Jack, he was a much better cook than I was, but that wasn't difficult. We finished off the casserole between us. I was absolutely stuffed.

"Oh, by the way," I said, after we'd finished eating. "I met your replacement today."

"What's he like?"

"We didn't get off to a very good start, and it's all your fault."

"My fault? How come? I left him a note telling him to go easy on you."

"Why didn't you tell me what his name was?"

"I did. I've mentioned it several times."

"Yeah, but I thought you said, Lee O'Reilly."

"I *did* say Leo Reilly."

"But I heard that as Lee. O. Reilly. Not Leo Riley. I thought he might be Irish."

"He's a Brummie."

"I know that now. I made a right fool of myself. I kept

calling him Mr O'Reilly."

Jack burst out laughing.

"It's not funny."

"It really is. What do you mean he gave you a hard time?"

"Just that. He came in specifically to say he didn't care who I was, or who I was in a relationship with, he didn't want me anywhere near any of his cases."

"That doesn't sound very promising. I'm sorry, Jill. It doesn't look like the note I left him did any good. If he's too hard on you, let me know."

"So you can do what? Stick up for me? I'm a big girl. I can look after myself. If I can handle you, I can handle him. I'm sure he'll grow to love me, eventually.

"Fair enough. Anyway, look, there's something I meant to mention to you earlier."

"What's that?"

"One of the guys from Washbridge station called to ask if I wanted to go bowling tonight."

"Did he now? So *that's* why you made dinner."

"No, of course not."

"Liar. You made dinner to butter me up so you could go bowling."

"I don't have to ask your permission."

"I know you don't, but it's rather curious that you would choose the same day to make dinner. Anyway, yeah, you should go."

He checked his watch. "I'm actually meant to be there in thirty minutes, so I really need to get going now."

"Sure, why not?"

"So you don't mind doing the dishes?"

Oh bum! I hadn't thought about the dishes. The sink

was stacked high with pots, pans and all manner of cutlery. Jack was a good cook, but he had a habit of using every pot and pan in the place.

"Err—yeah. It's okay, I guess. You get off."

He rushed upstairs, got changed, and then gave me a peck on the cheek.

"See you later."

"Yeah. Have a nice time."

I stared at the mountain of washing up. It would take me ages to do that lot. Unless, of course—

A little magic was called for.

During the six months we'd lived together, I'd been ultra-careful not to use magic in Jack's presence unless it had been unavoidable—an emergency of some kind. This was definitely an emergency—a washing-up emergency. It was his fault anyway; he'd been the one who'd said we couldn't afford a dishwasher. The 'take-it-back' spell wouldn't normally have been strong enough, but with my added powers, I was able to increase its scope so it went even further back. As soon as I'd cast the spell, the pots, pans and all the cutlery had reverted to their state before Jack used them. They were all sparkling clean. All I had to do was put them away.

"Jill?"

Oh bum!

"I forgot my car keys. Have you seen them?" Jack shouted from the hallway.

Oh, bum, bum, bum!

I rushed to the kitchen door to try and intercept him, but it was too late he was already inside.

"Jill, have you seen my—" He stared at the sink. "What—huh—how?"

"Your keys? Yeah, they're in there." I pointed to the bowl on the kitchen table.

"Right, thanks." He picked up the keys, and looked again at the sink. "How did you — ?"

I cast the 'forget' spell.

"Hurry up, Jack, or you'll be late for bowling."

I ushered him out of the door.

"Yeah, okay then. Bye."

Stupid! Stupid! Stupid! There was no excuse for what I'd just done. It had been laziness — plain and simple. I should have sucked it up and got stuck into the pot washing. Instead, I'd been forced to use magic on Jack — something I'd promised myself I would only do in a 'real' emergency.

When I walked into the living room, I felt a chill. There was a ghost in the room with me, but they weren't showing themselves. Somehow, I could sense that it wasn't my mother or the colonel.

"Hello? I know you're there. Please, attach yourself to me, so I can see and talk to you."

"Jill." The voice was very faint; I could barely make it out.

"Who is it? Do I know you?"

"Jill, can you hear me?"

The voice was so quiet that I couldn't even tell if it was a man or a woman.

"I'm here. Please show yourself so I can see you."

"Jill, can you hear me?"

"Yes, I can hear you."

But then the chill lifted, and the voice was gone. Whoever it was obviously knew me. But who was it?

Chapter 8

"Jill, can I have a word, please?" Jules collared me as soon as I walked into the office the next morning. She was red in the face, and looked close to tears.

Oh boy. Another great start to the day.

"Yes, Jules, what seems to be the matter?"

"It's Mrs V."

I had a feeling it might be. "What exactly is the problem?"

"She's taken my magazines and makeup out of the desk drawers, and slung them in the cupboard."

"I'm sure she didn't *sling* them in there."

"It isn't fair, Jill. We're meant to be sharing this job, so I think it's only right that we share the desk, too. I thought I would have all the drawers on the right-hand side, and Mrs V could have all the drawers on the left."

"That does sound fair, but did you actually sit down and discuss it with her?"

"No. We're not here on the same days."

"Mrs V did mention that you'd moved her crochet and patterns. It would probably have been better to speak to her first."

"How can I speak to her when I'm not here at the same time as her? Surely it's fair to have half the desk each."

"Look, I need to have a think about this. Leave it with me for a day or two. I'll sort something out that you can both live with."

"Okay, I suppose."

I was about to make my escape when Jules called me back.

"Could I ask your advice about something, Jill?"

"Sure. What is it?"

"It's about a guy, actually."

Who would have thought that I'd ever be asked for advice on matters of the heart?

"I've got a new boyfriend. His name's Gilbert. We've only been seeing one another for a few days. He's very nice—" She hesitated.

"I can sense a 'but' coming."

"But he's got a bit of acne at the moment."

"I don't think you can hold that against him. Lots of young people have acne. It's only a phase. Provided you like—"

"It's not that. I don't mind the acne."

"What's the problem, then?"

"He squeezes his spots."

"You should tell him not to do that. It could damage his skin."

"He even does it when he's out with me."

"Yuk!"

"I know. He does it all the time. We'll be sitting there in a bar, and all of a sudden his fingers go to his forehead."

"Gross! While you're out for a drink?"

"Yeah, and when we're eating too. We were in a restaurant last night; I'd just started on my dessert when—"

"Okay! Stop! I get the picture."

"If it was you, Jill, and you liked the guy, would you put up with the spot squeezing?"

"Honestly? No, I don't think I could get past that."

"You're right. I think I'll have to dump him. Thanks, Jill."

***

A chill fell in my office just as it had done the previous day at my house, but once again no-one appeared. This was very weird. Over the months, I'd developed a sense of when a ghost was around. It wasn't only the chill; there was something else too. Call it a sixth sense if you like, but something told me I wasn't alone in the room.

"Hey!" Winky jumped onto my desk. "Am I going to get any salmon today, or what?"

"Just a minute, Winky. I think there's a ghost in here."

"Do I look like I care? I could die of starvation while you're playing ghost hunter."

"I don't have any red."

"What? Why not?"

"Because I'm not made of money. I've just moved into a new house; it's been an expensive time for me."

"Shush!" He put a paw to his lips. "Listen, what's that sound?"

"I don't hear anything."

"Wait," he said. "I know what it is. It's a tiny violin playing."

"I should have known better than to expect any sympathy from you."

"If you could only drum up some new clients, you wouldn't be in this predicament, and you'd be able to afford to keep me in the style to which I've become accustomed."

"Do you want the pink or not?"

"I suppose I'll have to make do. What about Bella? What's happening there?"

"I'm still working on it."

The truth was, I still hadn't come up with any bright ideas as to where Bella could live, but I couldn't tell Winky that.

The same thing happened several times during the day. A chill would fall over the office, but then a few minutes later, it would go back to normal. I couldn't shake the feeling that someone else was around. In the end, I decided to contact my mother's ghost. She appeared almost immediately—she was never far away. I asked if she'd been trying to get through earlier.

"No, dear. I've been busy spring cleaning. In fact, I've left Alberto dusting the ornaments, so I'd better get back because you know what men are like. He'll probably drop something."

If it wasn't my mother and it wasn't the colonel, who was it? If anybody would know what was going on, it would be Mad—librarian and Ghost Hunter extraordinaire. I hadn't seen her for a while, but I knew she'd moved out of her mum's house. Hardly surprising—Delilah was a nightmare, and who would want to live with Nails and his low-flying toenails? Mad's new place was on the way back to Smallwash, so I decided I wouldn't bother phoning her. I'd just drop by on the off-chance; if she wasn't in, nothing lost.

Mad now lived in a small block of flats in an area of Washbridge which was known for its high crime rate. But then, if anyone could handle herself, it was Mad. I doubted she'd lose any sleep over the area's reputation, and you could bet she was getting a good deal on the rent. As luck would have it, she was in when I arrived.

"Jill? What brings you here, stranger?"

"I hope you don't mind me dropping in unannounced like this."

"Not at all. I was beginning to think you'd fallen out with me."

"Of course not. It's just that I've been pretty busy."

"Come on in."

I'd no sooner stepped inside than something knocked me back against the door.

"Albert!" Mad shouted. "Get down! Come here!"

The invisible paws which had had me pinned to the door, released me.

"I'd forgotten you had Albert with you now."

"There isn't really enough room for him in here, but I couldn't leave him in Ghost Town any longer. Go and get in your basket," she ordered her invisible, ghost dog.

Inside, the flat was even smaller than I'd expected.

"It's very cosy."

"Don't you mean poky?"

"No. I just meant—"

"Of course it's poky, but it's all I can afford right now. A librarian's pay isn't great, and even though the ghost hunting helps, it doesn't add up to much. But I don't care how small this place is, it's better than living with my mother and that horrible boyfriend of hers."

"Is she still with Nails?"

"Yeah, she's smitten. I have no idea why."

"What about you? Are you seeing anyone?"

"I've been out with a couple of guys since I last saw you, but nothing that's lasted."

"It looks like you've settled in okay. I see you've made your mark on it."

"My mark? Cheek!" She laughed. "What you really

mean is I'm untidy."

"You are a bit."

"You know me, Jill. I'm not like you; I'm not all house and gardens."

"What do you mean? I'm not like that."

"Of course you are. Everything has to be just so. A place for everything, and everything in its place. Anyway, what brings you here? I get the feeling that this isn't just a social call."

"You're right, although I did want to see your place. Look, I don't know what's going on, but several times today there's been a chill in my office. The sort of chill I usually experience when my mother or the colonel is about to appear, but no one did. It's weird. It's like I can sense there's a ghost in there, but I can't see anyone. I checked with my mother; she said it wasn't her, and that she'd been spring cleaning all day. I couldn't get a hold of the colonel, but I don't think it was him. Any bright ideas about what might be going on?"

"I've heard of that sort of thing happening," Mad said. "It's usually when the ghost is hesitant or unable to make contact. It could be someone who's recently passed over, and is unsure of the whole 'attaching' thing."

"So you think someone is trying to contact me?"

"Probably, yes."

"Is there anything I can do to help them, or to at least find out who it is?"

"The only thing you can do is encourage them."

"How do I do that?"

"The next time you feel the chill and the sensation that there's a ghost in the room, talk to them."

"How can I talk to them if I don't know who it is?"

"Speak to them in general terms. Say something like: 'Welcome. Please show yourself.' That sort of thing. Try to make them feel that you want to see them."

"But what if it's someone I *don't* want to see? What if it's Battery?"

"It won't be Battery; he's banged up in prison in Ghost Town."

"But there are plenty of other characters I wouldn't want to meet. I've made a lot of enemies in this job."

"That's a risk you're going to have to take if you want to find out who it is."

"Okay. I'll have to give it some thought."

"Anyway, Jill, when are we going to have another night out?"

"Err—soon. Definitely soon. Jack and I have just moved into a new house, so we've got tons to do."

"I had no idea you had a new place."

"It's in Smallwash. You knew I'd been living at his flat, didn't you?"

"I assume that must have worked out okay seeing as you're still together?"

"It did—for the most part. It's just that flat of his. It was okay for the first month or so, but then it started to get to me. It was way too small."

"I bet it wasn't any smaller than this place."

"No, but then there are two of us. It wasn't just that. It never felt like my place, and his furniture drove me insane. The man's got no taste."

"I hope you didn't say that to him."

"I tell him all the time. It doesn't seem to bother him, and he's shown no sign of changing. Anyway, I managed to persuade him we needed to find somewhere new—

somewhere we could choose together. So that's what we did."

"Smallwash is over the river, isn't it?"

"Yeah."

"Do you have to go over that toll bridge?"

"Don't mention toll bridges to me."

***

"What do you want, Gooder?"

Inspector Maxine Jewell greeted me with her usual charm offensive. She was proof, if it was needed, that the Candlefield police were about as enamoured with me as their human world counterparts.

"I just need a quick word."

"I don't have time to talk to the likes of you."

"The likes of me?"

"Timewasters, troublemakers—shall I go on?"

"Okay, I get it. You're not a fan. But this will only take a minute."

"That's a minute too long."

"Would you rather I talked to The Candle?"

"About what? You might think you're something special because you were offered the chance to become a level seven witch, but let me tell you, it doesn't impress me. You have no right to conduct investigations here in Candlefield."

"I just wanted to ask you why the police are suppressing reports about the recent poisonings?"

The colour rose in her face. "What poisonings?"

"Two members of the Eagles' BoundBall team have obviously been poisoned, and yet, according to the police, it's some sort of virus."

"Presumably, that's what the hospital reported to us."

"Rubbish. They were told by your people to say it was a virus."

"I don't know what you're talking about, Gooder."

"Okay. Then you won't mind if I take this to The Candle. I can see the headline now: 'Police Cover Up Poisonings'."

"Wait." She looked around to make sure no one was listening. "This is strictly between you and me, okay?"

"I can't guarantee—"

"Just listen! It *was* a poisoning, but we can't make it public because if we do, there'll be a mass panic. The vampires will refuse to drink synthetic blood, and if they can't drink that, they'll go en masse to the human world in search of human blood. Do you want that on your conscience?"

I hadn't seen that coming. What Maxine had said actually made sense. If there was mass panic among the vampire population, it could be disastrous.

"Right. I see. I'm sorry."

"That's just it, Gooder. You think you know it all, but you don't. You haven't been here long enough. Something similar happened about thirty years ago. There was some kind of poisoning incident related to synthetic blood. Word got out, and there was carnage in the human world. So you see, this has to be kept under wraps."

"I understand. I won't say anything."

"And leave the investigation to us."

I wasn't about to promise that.

Chapter 9

It was JV Day, and I wasn't looking forward to the morning ahead of me. For most businesses, 'JV' would have stood for Joint Venture, but not for me. JV stood for Jules and Mrs V. I'd asked Jules to come in on her day off because it was time for me to get things resolved once and for all, before the two of them came to blows, or drove me insane.

As soon as I walked into the outer office, I realised that it wasn't going to be easy. Mrs V was behind her desk, knitting, and deliberately not looking at Jules, who was sitting on a chair on the other side of the office, near to the linen basket. Jules was busy doing something on her phone, but again, deliberately not looking at Mrs V. It seemed that all of my powers of diplomacy were going to be required.

What do you mean, I don't have any?

"Morning, ladies!"

"Morning, Jill." Mrs V still refused to look at Jules.

"Morning, Jill," Jules said, without looking up from her phone.

"Okay you two, we need to sort this out if you're going to continue to job share."

"*I* don't have a problem," Mrs V said. She glanced at Jules. "If a certain someone would respect my desk, there wouldn't be an issue."

Before I could say anything, Jules jumped in. "Just a minute, I'm meant to be sharing this job, so I don't think it's unreasonable to expect to share the desk."

"I've had this desk for more years than you've been alive, young lady. I was working for Jill's father when Jill was still in nappies."

"What am I supposed to do with my stuff? I've got to put it somewhere."

I stepped in before Mrs V told Jules exactly where she could put her stuff.

"We've already been down this road, and it hasn't got us anywhere. We need to talk this through like adults. Jules, will you shuffle your chair over here?"

She wheeled it over so that she was next to Mrs V's desk. The two of them were looking daggers at one another.

"Mrs V, you approached me to say that working five days a week was getting a little too much for you, didn't you?"

"Yes, but I'm beginning to think that was a mistake. Maybe I should go back to five days."

"No, sorry. There's no going back now that I've taken Jules on. I can hardly throw her out, can I?"

Mrs V glared at Jules, and I could sense that she wanted to ask why not, but she bit her tongue — thank goodness.

After a few moments, I continued. "We have to find a way to make this job share work. Mrs V, wouldn't you say that if you're sharing a job, it's only fair you share the desk? After all, when you're not here, Jules does have to sit there."

"Yes, and I don't have a problem with that. What I *do* have a problem with is people moving my things around without asking first."

"I can understand that. Jules, don't you think it would have been polite to ask Mrs V if she minded you sharing half the desk, before moving her things?"

"Yeah, I guess so, but she wasn't here for me to ask, was

she?"

"Okay, let's see what we've established so far. Mrs V, you're happy to share the desk. And Jules, you realise you should have asked before moving Mrs V's stuff. Is that right?"

They both nodded.

"Okay, in that case, why don't we turn back the clock and pretend none of this happened. Jules, you're in the office with Mrs V now. What would you like to ask her?"

Jules hesitated for a moment. I could tell she was a little intimidated by Mrs V, but she managed to summon up the courage.

"Mrs V?" her voice wavered a little.

"Yes, young lady?" Mrs V wasn't going to make this easy for her.

"Seeing as how we're now job sharing, and I have to use your desk when you're not here —"

"Yes?"

"Do you think that we could possibly share the drawers, so that you have half and I have half?"

Mrs V glanced at me, and took a deep breath. "Yes, that's perfectly acceptable to me, but I'd like a day to rearrange my things, so I know where everything is. I'll leave one set of drawers empty; that can be your side."

"That sounds fair, doesn't it, Jules?" I said, with my fingers crossed.

"Yeah, I'm happy with that."

"But —" Mrs V hadn't finished. "Once I've done that, I don't expect to find your things in my half of the desk. Understood?"

"Yeah, no problem."

"And, young lady, I do not expect to find my desktop a

mess, I don't want to see smudges of makeup on it."

"I wouldn't do that."

"Or tea stains."

Oh dear. Jules was renowned for spilling drinks.

"If I do spill anything, I'll make sure I wipe it up, so it's as good as new."

That was my cue to step in again. "Right, we seem to have reached an agreement. Mrs V will move her things out of one side of the desk today, ready for when you come in tomorrow. Are we all agreed?"

They both nodded.

"Right, Jules, off you go then. I'll pay you for your time today."

I could still feel the tension between them as I walked through to my office, but at least we'd cleared the air, and made some sort of agreement. I'd just have to see how long the uneasy truce lasted.

An hour later, I thought I'd better check how things were going. Mrs V had piles of her stuff on top of the desk.

"Is everything all right, Mrs V?"

"I'll never get all of this in one side."

"You could always use the cupboard behind you."

"I suppose I'll have to."

"Good, oh and by the way, I'm expecting the accountant any time now."

"I don't know how you expect me to do this, *and* see to your visitors."

***

Luther Stone was every bit as hot as I remembered him.

"Luther, nice to see you."

"You too, Jill. We've missed you. That apartment block is not the same without you; I don't know why you had to go and leave us."

"You know why. I moved in with Jack."

"Why couldn't he have moved in with you?"

"With hindsight, I wish he had. I hate that poky flat of his, but anyway, we've moved out now. We've got a house in Smallwash."

"Really? How long have you been living there?"

"Only a few days. You'll never guess who I saw."

"Mr Ivers?"

"How did you know?"

"When you mentioned Smallwash, I realised you must have to go over the toll bridge. Mr Ivers likes to keep me updated on his life—such as it is. He told me a few weeks back that he had a new job. He made it sound like it was something really exciting. When I eventually found out what it was—taking fees on the toll bridge at Smallwash—I almost died laughing. Never was anyone more suited to a job."

"I couldn't believe it." I laughed. "I honestly thought I'd got rid of him and his newsletters. He's saved all the back issues for me. All twenty-four of them!"

"Oh dear." Luther grinned. "Poor you. But then, if I have to put up with him, I don't see why you shouldn't. Anyway, I suppose I should take a look at your books."

"I doubt they'll look much better than the last time you were here. Business has been very slow. Before you start, how are you and Betty getting along?"

"Didn't you know? We've split up."

"Really? I had no idea. Is she still living there?"

"Yeah, it's a bit awkward, really. I see her every day, so as you can imagine, there's a bit of an atmosphere."

"What happened if you don't mind me asking?"

"It was stupid really. We had an argument over starfish."

"The reality TV celebrity who was murdered?"

"What?"

"Sorry. Just a case I worked on. So you fell out over a starfish? How did you manage that?"

"Like I said, it was stupid. We were at a seashell fair, and were both looking around the stalls to see if we could find anything to add to our collections. I spotted a fabulous specimen, and was just about to pay for it when Betty snatched it, and bought it for herself."

"What did you say?"

"I told her I was just about to buy it. She said, 'You snooze you lose'."

"Charming."

"I know. I couldn't believe it."

"Betty does have a dark side. I've seen it myself."

"We had a big argument on the way home, which spiralled out of control. In the end, we both decided it was probably best to call it a day."

"I'm really sorry. But I always thought you two made — err — an unusual couple."

"I suppose we did."

"Are you still into sea creatures?"

"To be honest, Jill, that incident kind of spoiled it for me. It's a pity because I was really getting into it in a big way. It can be quite exciting, you know."

"I'll have to take your word for that."

"Anyway, after that day, I kind of lost the heart for it."

"Maybe that's for the best, I never really did see you as a seashell kind of a guy."

***

I'd arranged to drop into another jeweller, All That Glitters, to see if their story was the same as the others. Ethan Moore, the manager, was only too happy to talk me through what happened. It was almost word for word what I'd heard on the previous two occasions. He too had a CCTV recording of the 'incident' and invited me to view it.

"What's that on the floor, close to the door?" I pointed to the screen.

"We were having some work done to extend the shop. Even though it was boarded up, the plaster dust was everywhere. That area to the side of the door was the worst affected because it was closest to where they were working."

After Ethan had zoomed in, I could see a number of footprints in the plaster dust. He zoomed back out, and we continued to watch the recording. The assistant behind the counter was showing a tray full of rings to an elderly couple. One moment the tray was full of jewellery, the next it was empty. The pattern was exactly the same as I'd seen with the two other thefts.

At my request, he allowed the recording to play for a few more moments, and then stopped it. I asked him to zoom in on the area next to the door again. There, in the dust, was one extra set of footprints, and yet no one had come into or out of the shop. Where had those footprints come from?

I'd asked Alan to arrange for me to meet with the Eagles' team captain; a young man named Eddie Wonder. Eddie had movie star looks, and one of those smiles that could melt a girl's—err—heart. Not that I'd noticed, obviously.

We met at the team's clubhouse; Alan came along with me.

"Nice to meet you, Jill." Eddie's smile almost blinded me.

"Thanks for seeing me."

"No problem," he said. "The sooner we get this sorted out, the better. The players are dropping like flies at the moment. I'm not sure how we're going to field a team."

"I know it's an obvious question, but do you have any idea who might be behind this? Who would want to weaken the team in this way?"

"Oh yes, I don't have any doubt who's behind it. It's obviously the Blue Flags."

"Blue Flags?"

"They're our main opposition. We're in second place in the league at the moment; the Blue Flags are in first. Effectively, whoever wins the match between our two teams is more or less guaranteed to win the league, so there's a lot at stake."

"Do you think they may be trying to sabotage your team?"

"I don't think it, I know it. I wouldn't put anything past them. Their team captain is absolutely ruthless."

"What's his name?"

"Teddy Barr."

"What about you, Alan?" I asked. "Do you think that's a

possibility?"

"I don't know." Alan shrugged. "To be honest, I've always got on well with Teddy. He's a bit loud, and he's certainly a bighead, but I couldn't see him doing anything like this."

"You've always been naïve, Alan," Eddie said. "Of course he would. If it meant they'd win the league, he'd do it in a heartbeat."

"Do you know where I can find Teddy Barr?"

"I've got his contact details," Alan said. "I'll give them to you afterwards."

We talked for a while longer. Eddie was mainly interested in telling me all about his achievements as team captain. He might have been a good-looking guy, but boy, was he boring.

After Eddie had left, I walked to Cuppy C with Alan.

"What did you make of Eddie?" he asked.

"He was a bit full of himself. Is he always like that?"

"Yeah. He can be a bit full-on. You'd never think his fiancée had just dumped him, would you?"

"Why did she do that?"

"No idea. They'd been together for ages. They'd even set a date for the wedding, but then she just called it off."

As I saw it, there were two lines of enquiry I needed to follow up on. I had to find out more about the service which delivered the synthetic blood, and I also needed to speak with the captain of the Blue Flags, Teddy Barr.

Chapter 10

I was on my way up to the office when I bumped into my landlord, Zac.

"Hi, Jill."

"Hey, Zac. How's it going?"

"Much better now I've got rid of Gordon Armitage. I imagine you were sorry to see him go?"

"Oh yeah. Devastated."

"I owe you a favour, Jill. If it hadn't been for you holding out, I think I would've had him as a permanent tenant, and to be honest, he was much more trouble than he was worth. The man never stopped complaining. There wasn't a week went by when he didn't ring me up about something. I was glad to see the back of him."

"Me too. Any idea who's going to be taking the space he vacated?"

"Funny you should ask that because we signed a contract earlier today. Your new neighbours should be moving in anytime now."

"Can you tell me who it is?"

"Yeah, it's no secret. It's a business called I-Sweat."

"I-Sweat? I'm not sure I like the sound of that. What kind of business is it?"

"It's a health club—gym—that sort of thing. That's why it's taken a while to sort out. They want to make some structural changes—knock a few of the offices into one big room. They've signed a long lease, so I'm happy to go along with their plans."

"It's certainly quite a change from Armitage, Armitage, Armitage and Poole. When they're open, maybe I'll pop in there on my lunch hour. I need to get myself in shape."

"You look in good shape to me."

"Well thank you, kind sir."

"Any news on Bella?" Winky said, as soon as I walked through the door.

Sheesh! My life wasn't my own.

"Not yet, but I'm still working on it. Don't worry, I'll get it sorted for you."

He didn't look convinced.

Just then, the room became chilly. The ghost, whoever it was, was trying to get through to me again.

"Hello, Jill? Can you hear me?"

"Yes, I'm here. Please attach yourself to me so I can see you."

"I'm trying to. Just give me a second." The voice was a little stronger today. For the first time, I could tell it was definitely a man, but I still didn't know who it was. But then, suddenly, a blast of pure energy knocked me back in my seat. When I recovered, there was a figure standing in front of me. He'd done it; he'd broken through.

"Dad?"

It was my birth father. The last time I'd seen him had been over a year ago when he'd tried to save me from Drake—from TDO. And in doing so, he'd lost his own life. For several weeks after his death, I'd hoped that his ghost would appear, but there had been no sign. I'd even asked my mother, but she hadn't seen him. In the end, I'd come to the conclusion that he'd elected to bypass Ghost Town. But I'd been wrong because there he was—standing in front of me.

"That was hard work." He gasped. "Being a ghost is a lot more difficult than being alive."

"Dad, where have you been?"

"I've been dead." He grinned.

"I know that. I mean why didn't you come back earlier?"

"I wasn't sure if I'd be welcome. I wasn't a very good father to you. I abandoned you when you needed me most."

"No. You *came back* when I needed you most."

"I didn't do much good though, did I?"

"Of course you did. I doubt I'd be standing here now, if you hadn't tried to warn me about Drake."

"I never would have forgiven myself if TDO had killed you. How are you?"

"I'm fine, but what about you?"

"I'm still trying to get used to this ghost lark. I'm not very good at it as you've probably gathered. At least now that I've managed to get through once, it should be easier next time. That's if you want to see me again?"

"Of course I do. You're my dad."

"Not a very good one."

"You can make up for that now, can't you?"

"Yes, I'd like that. If you'll let me."

"Of course I will. I like the idea of you being around."

"That's great. I really wasn't sure how you'd react. Look, this really is terribly exhausting. I suppose it'll get better when I've had more practice. I'm going to have to love you and leave you for now."

"Okay. Bye, Dad."

With that, he disappeared. Maybe I would be able to get to know my birth father after all. Better dead than never.

***

It was quiet in Cuppy C. The twins were both behind the counter in the tea room while one of their assistants was looking after the cake shop.

"You two are looking remarkably pleased with yourselves," I said.

"We are, and would you like to know why?"

"Go on then, and you can get me a blueberry muffin while you're telling me."

"You'll have to pay for it, Jill." Amber huffed. "When you used to work behind the counter for us we didn't mind you having the odd free one, but I can't remember the last time you were behind here."

"That's fair enough. If you ever get stuck and need any help, you can still give me a shout, but otherwise I don't really see the point. I'm very busy—you know how it is. I've got lots of cases to solve."

"Here you are." Amber passed me the muffin. "You can still have staff discount."

"How much is that? Seventy percent?"

"Twenty." Pearl took my money.

"Do I get a free cup of tea or do I have to pay for that as well?"

"Go on then. You can have a cup of tea."

"So, are you going to tell me why you two are so happy?"

"We've let the two rooms upstairs."

"Since when?"

"Since this morning."

"It would have been nice to have been consulted."

"What do you mean?" Pearl said. "It's our shop; they're our rooms."

"Yeah I know they are, but have you forgotten that there are three rooms upstairs, and I live in one of them? It would have been nice to at least see the people that you're taking on as my new roommates."

"How could we have done that?" Amber said. "We couldn't call you over every time somebody came in to view them. Don't you trust our judgment?"

"Not particularly. Do the words 'chocolate fountain' and 'conveyor belt' ring a bell?"

"That's totally different. Anyway, you can't talk. At least no one mistakes Cuppy C for a tanning salon."

The two of them dissolved into laughter.

"Can I get a discount on a spray tan?" Amber managed through her tears.

"Very funny. Who told you about that?"

"Grandma, who do you think? She's been telling everyone."

Great!

"Anyway." Pearl finally managed to compose herself. "You'll like the people who are moving in."

"Who are they?"

"Two witches: Laura and Flora."

"No, seriously, what are their real names?"

"Those are their real names. Honestly."

"Are they related to one another?"

"No, they're just good friends. They'd hoped to get a flat of their own but they couldn't afford it, so when they saw these rooms, it was the next best thing. They're really nice, Jill. I'm sure you'll like them."

"I don't really have much choice do I?"

"Stop moaning and eat your muffin."

The twins were right. I wasn't in any position to dictate who they could and couldn't rent the rooms out to because, after all, I was still getting my room rent-free. The original arrangement had been that I'd help out in the shop in return for the room, but in all honesty, I'd grown tired of working in Cuppy C. And, although I hated to admit it, I was pretty useless behind the counter.

I'd been so busy talking to the twins that I hadn't noticed Daze. She'd pulled two tables together in the far corner of the shop. Seated around them were a number of Rogue Retrievers. I recognised Blaze, Haze and Maze. Normally, I would have gone over and said hello, but I could see that they were holding some kind of meeting, and I didn't like to interrupt. There were raised voices, and strong words were obviously being exchanged. I decided it was best to leave them to it, so I found a table next to the window.

Miles and Mindy had been remarkably quiet of late which was a little disconcerting. For a short period, immediately after Grandma had taken pity on him, he'd pretended to be Mr Nice Guy. That hadn't lasted long; he'd soon reverted to type. There were no second chances for him. This time, Grandma had dropped the hammer on his wool shop, and ever since then he'd been trying to get even by targeting Cuppy C. But the twins and I were wise to his games, and so far nothing had come of his little pranks. Still, if I knew Miles, he wouldn't let things lie.

The sound of chairs and tables being pushed across the floor signalled the end of Daze's meeting. Blaze gave me a quick wave on his way out. Daze, who was now by herself, caught my eye and beckoned me over.

"That meeting looked very serious." I took the seat

opposite her.

"It was. We have something of a problem, but I'd prefer it didn't get out."

"You can tell me. My lips are sealed."

"One of Candlefield's most notorious villains broke out of prison a few weeks ago."

"Who's that?"

"A wizard, known by the nickname: Stopwatch."

"Strange name. I assume there's a reason for it?"

"Occasionally, a wizard or a witch will devise a totally new spell that has never been seen before. Generally, that's something to be celebrated because it adds to the combined knowledge of the magic community. But not if the wizard or witch has evil intentions."

"I'm guessing Stopwatch falls into that category?"

"You'd be right. Stopwatch was a criminal long before he came up with the spell that he's best known for."

"What is the spell, exactly?"

"As the name suggests it has to do with time. Stopwatch concocted a spell which can halt time."

"What exactly do you mean by that?"

"When he casts the spell, time stands still. Everything around him stops dead, but he is able to move around and operate as normal."

"Do you have any idea where he is?"

"We're almost certain he's in Washbridge. The problem isn't locating him; it's how to catch him. The 'stopwatch' spell from which he gets his nickname is very powerful. He's the only one who knows how to cast it, and the only one who can reverse it. Whenever we get near to him, he casts the spell, and makes his getaway while we're frozen in time."

"How did you ever get him into prison in the first place?"

"Luckily for us, Stopwatch enjoys a drink. Back then, we caught him in a drunken stupor, and managed to clamp him with anti-magic shackles."

"Anti-magic what?"

"They prevent a witch or wizard from casting spells. They're rarely used—only in cases where a wizard or witch is able to perform a spell which cannot be counteracted by the guards."

"How did he manage to break out?"

"A new guard was on duty in the cell block where Stopwatch was being held. For reasons that are beyond me, he hadn't been warned of Stopwatch's particular powers, and was totally unaware of the purpose of the shackles. It's a disgrace. Whoever is in charge should be sacked. Anyway, Stopwatch managed to convince the guard to remove the shackles. As soon as they were off, Stopwatch cast the spell, and halted time. That allowed him to take the guard's key, let himself out of the cell, and just walk out of the prison. He hasn't been seen since."

"I can see why there were so many Rogue Retrievers here."

"We're all heading over to Washbridge to see if we can flush him out. I'd better get going, Jill. Nice to see you again."

"Okay, Daze, keep in touch. Good luck."

Listening to Daze talk about Stopwatch had given me an idea. It was a long shot, but worth a punt.

Chapter 11

I was munching on my cornflakes. Jack wasn't much of a morning person, so we rarely had any in-depth conversations before work—more a series of grunts. Over the previous six months, I'd got so that I could recognise his various grunts, and now had a pretty good idea of what he was saying.

"Jill, I've been thinking."

"Yeah?"

"I think we should have a housewarming party."

I hated parties; any kind of party. Birthday, Christmas, Anniversary? They were all the same. Lots of noisy people, eating and drinking too much.

"Do people still have housewarming parties? Aren't they a bit noughties?"

"Of course they do. It will be great to have all of our friends around."

What friends?

"And relatives. Kathy and Peter and the kids would love it."

"Kids? In my house?"

"*Our* house."

"Yeah. Our house—that's what I meant. It would be much too boring for the kids."

"Rubbish. Kathy told me that Lizzie can't wait to see her auntie's new house. I could invite my friends from Washbridge station—some of them will have kids too."

The thought of kids running wild in my brand new house made me want to weep.

"It's only a small house. Think of the mess."

"There's plenty of room. So what if they drop a few

crumbs on the floor as long as everyone has a good time?"

"A few crumbs? The place will be wrecked."

"You're overreacting as usual."

"I'm not overreacting! When did I ever overreact? Never, that's when. I've never overreacted in my life. Not once. Not ever."

He laughed, which really got my back up.

"And of course, we'd have to invite your birth family."

"Why?"

"What do you mean 'why'? Because they're your family, and they'll want to see your new house."

"No they won't. They hate houses. Especially other people's. They're always telling me how much they hate houses. And parties. And they really hate parties in houses. Besides, they live too far away."

"Where exactly is it they live?"

"I've told you. Up north."

"Up north where? The North Pole?"

"Don't be stupid."

"You're the one who's being stupid. Or obstinate, at least. You have to invite your birth family, or I'll make it my business to track them down, and invite them myself."

Oh bum!

"Okay, okay. I'll invite them. So when are we going to do this? In a few months' time? What about next summer?"

"No, the whole point of a housewarming party is that you hold it just after you've moved in. I thought maybe this weekend."

"This weekend? Great."

***

"What's wrong, Jill?" Jules said, as soon as I walked into the office.

"Don't ask."

"You and Jack haven't fallen out, have you?"

"Not yet, but we're probably going to. He wants a housewarming party."

"How exciting! Do I get an invite?"

Me and my big mouth.

"Yeah, I suppose so. If we ever get around to it."

"I love parties."

You and everyone else, apparently.

I walked through to my office. I'd have to be careful not to mention the housewarming in front of Winky, or he'd want to come too. It was bad enough having a houseful of people; I didn't want cats too.

There were six or seven cats, all sitting on the floor. They were all looking at Winky who was perched on my desk. I glared at him, but he totally ignored me. Such was the power I had over him.

"Okay, you guys." He addressed his audience. "Do you all know what your jobs are?"

They all nodded.

"Right, let's get to it. We'll meet at the same time tomorrow. If you have any problems, just give me a call. Okay?"

"Okay, boss," they all chorused.

The next thing I knew, they all hurried out of the window — onto the ledge, and out of sight.

"Where are they going? They'll kill themselves."

"Don't be ridiculous. They know what they're doing."

"Who are they, anyway?"

"That's FCF."

"What's that when it's at home?"

"Feline Crime Fighters."

"What does FCF have to do with you?"

"I'm the founder member."

"And what exactly does FCF do?"

"Surprisingly, it fights crime. The clue's in the name."

"How long has it been in operation?"

"It's relatively new. It's probably escaped your notice because you humans are too wrapped up in your own world, but there's been a big increase in feline crime activity over the last six months."

"Feline crime? I didn't realise that was a thing."

"Which just goes to prove my point. You humans are totally self-absorbed."

"Who's responsible for fighting feline crime?"

"Who do you think? The police, of course."

"Feline police?"

"You don't think the human police would care, do you?"

"I'm still trying to get my head around this. Are you saying there's a feline police force?"

"Of course there is, and feline fire and ambulance services."

"Why don't you let the feline police deal with the crime wave?"

"That's rich coming from you. The feline police force is useless."

"What are you planning to do about it?"

"We're going to bring the criminals to justice ourselves."

"You mean like vigilantes?"

"How are we any more a vigilante than you?"

"People pay me to solve cases."

"Who says we aren't being paid? Do you think I'm doing this out of the goodness of my heart?"

I should have realised. Winky wasn't in this to clean up the streets; he was in it just to clean up. This cat never missed a trick.

"If you need any help from a professional—"

"Why? Do you know one?"

"Cheek! Do you think I could have my desk back?"

"For now, but if things start to get busy, I may have to commandeer it, and you'll have to find somewhere else to work."

"In case you hadn't noticed, it's my name on the building."

"Yeah, I meant to ask you, what's with those horrible colours? White text on orange? It looks like a tanning salon."

***

I'd arranged to meet with the owners of all the jewellery shops that had been targeted by the thief. We were in the back office of 'Are Forever'.

"Gentlemen, thank you for agreeing to meet with me today."

"Have you made any progress?" Ethan said.

"It's possible I may have, but I can't go into any detail just yet because it may jeopardise my enquiry. For me to pursue this further, I'll need the cooperation of all of you."

"What do you want us to do?" Arnold said.

"After talking to each of you, and viewing the CCTV,

one thing has come to my attention. Whoever is committing these crimes is a creature of habit. The thefts follow a well-defined pattern. After comparing the time stamps on all the CCTV coverage, I've noticed that the thefts all took place on either a Tuesday or a Thursday, and always at precisely two pm."

"That much is obvious to anyone, but how does that help us if we can't see who's doing it?"

"Like I said, I can't go into details because that may jeopardise my plans, but I'm pretty confident that I'll be able to capture this thief. But to do that, I'm going to need to lay a trap for him. I can only do that if you all agree to work with me. This Tuesday, I want you all to close shop at approximately quarter to two. All of you except Arnold, that is. Are Forever must remain open."

"Just a minute." One of the other owners objected. "We can't afford to close."

"You'll only need to close for thirty minutes."

"Why does my shop remain open?" Arnold asked.

"Because if the thief is still operating in this area, and I believe he is, then I fully expect him to hit another shop at the same time this Tuesday. If your shop is the only one open, then he'll have no choice but to choose yours."

"But surely he'll realise that someone might have spotted a pattern by now, or that it's a trap?"

"Why would he care? He knows no one can see him. When he strikes, I'll be waiting."

"Look, Jill, I'm probably being a bit slow here," Arnold said. "Even if what you said is true, and you know for sure he's going to target my shop at two o'clock this Tuesday, I still don't understand how you're going to catch him, because he seems to be invisible."

"I have my methods. Will you all trust me, and give me your support?"

Somewhat reluctantly, they all agreed to play along. It was apparent that they didn't have a great deal of confidence in my plan.

I couldn't blame them—neither did I.

***

My phone rang; it was Kathy. She sounded *way* too excited.

"I just wanted to let you know that we'll definitely be coming."

"That's nice. Coming where?"

"To your housewarming party, of course."

Oh bum!

"Jack rang me earlier."

I was going to kill him.

"That's great. When is it you'll be coming?"

"It's *your* housewarming, Jill. Surely, you know when it is?"

"Of course I know. I just don't have my diary with me."

"Jack said it was this Sunday."

"*This* Sunday?"

"The kids are really looking forward to it. Jack said there would be other kids there, too."

"Did he?" Great!

"Who else is coming?"

"No one much. We're going to keep it a small affair."

"That's not the impression Jack gave me. What about your birth family? You have to invite the twins over, and it would be great to finally meet your aunt Lucy."

"I think they're all doing something that day."

"Come on Jill, you can't hide them away forever. Anybody would think you're ashamed of them."

"Of course I'm not." I knocked the phone against my arm. "Oh dear, the line is breaking up. Sorry, Kathy, I'll get back to you later."

Jack had a cheek. He'd only mentioned the idea that morning, and yet he'd already told Kathy about it. He'd done it deliberately because he knew I'd try and put it off forever. What was I supposed to do now? What would I say when he asked me to invite my birth family over?

Oh bum!

Chapter 12

"Jill? It's Pearl."

"Hi, Pearl. Is everything okay?"

"Yes, everything's fine. It's just that the two girls who are moving in upstairs are here, and we thought you might like to pop over to meet them."

"Right now?"

"Yeah, if you're not too busy."

"Sure, okay. I'll be there in a couple of minutes."

Before I could magic myself over to Candlefield, Winky jumped onto my desk.

"There's still no sign of you sorting out this problem with Bella. Have you forgotten about it?"

"Of course not. I'm still working very hard on it."

"You could have fooled me."

"I promise. It's number one on my priority list."

"Show me."

"Show you what?"

"Your priority list."

"There isn't *actually* a list."

"You just said there was."

"It's a metaphorical list."

"If you don't get this sorted, and Bella leaves, you're going to regret it."

"I've told you. It's in hand."

"It had better be or you will feel my wrath, and I don't mean my metaphorical wrath."

What else was I meant to tell him? Right now, the situation looked pretty hopeless, but he definitely didn't want to hear that.

I magicked myself over to Cuppy C. The twins were at a window table with two other young witches.

"Jill." Pearl pulled up a chair for me. "This is Flora and Laura — your new roommates."

Flora and Laura were like two book-ends. Both had dirty blonde hair, both wore way too much makeup, and neither of them had any dress-sense. Not that I was judging.

"Hi, lovely to meet you both."

What? Who are you calling two-faced?

"Hi, I'm Flora." She was the taller of the two. I shook her hand; it was icy cold.

"I'm Laura." Laura's hand was also cold. What was it with these ice maidens?

"Do you like your rooms?"

"Oh, yes." Flora beamed. "We've been looking for somewhere suitable for months now, but all the flats are too expensive, and all the rooms we've seen have been horrible. But these are lovely."

"Do you both work in Candlefield?"

"I do," Flora said. "I work in the flower shop in the market square."

"That's quite appropriate." I grinned.

She looked puzzled.

"Flora? Flowers? Plants?"

She still looked puzzled. Oh boy.

"Never mind. What about you, Laura?"

"I work in a shop in Washbridge."

"Oh? Which one?"

"Ashleys. We sell home furnishings. It's a few doors down from the library."

"I know where you mean. What made you decide to work in the human world?"

"I just fancied a change."

"How do you like it?"

"To be honest, I prefer working with sups. I'm looking for a job back in Candlefield."

"How do you two know one another?"

"We've known each other practically all our lives, haven't we Flora?"

"Yes, we met at school, and we've been friends ever since."

"Have the twins told you anything about me?"

"They didn't need to," Flora said. "Everyone has heard of the great Jill Gooder. You're the witch who turned down the chance to go to level seven."

"And you killed TDO," Laura added. "How could we not know about you?"

"Yeah, well. I only popped over to say hello. I'd better get back to Washbridge because I'm working on a few cases at the moment. It was nice to meet you both."

"You too, bye."

"See you soon."

I had to admit it. The twins had been right about my new roommates. Apart from their cold hands and lack of any dress sense, it was difficult to fault them. And with a bit of luck, they wouldn't be at each other's throats all the time like the twins were.

***

It had taken me a while, but I'd finally managed to get hold of Teddy Barr on the phone. We'd arranged to meet in a small café in Candlefield market square.

"I've heard a lot about you," he said. Teddy didn't have Eddie Wonder's movie star looks, but he exuded the same self-confidence. "You're meant to be the most powerful witch in Candlefield."

"That's what some people say."

"So, what does the most powerful witch in Candlefield want with a mere vampire?"

"I wanted to speak to you in your capacity as captain of the Blue Flags BoundBall team."

"I wouldn't have had you down as a BoundBall fan, although now I come to think about it, didn't you organise that women's game?"

"I did, yes."

"What are you after? Free tickets for the big game? I can get you a few of those—no problem."

"No, nothing like that. Have you heard that two of the Eagles' players have been taken ill?"

"Yeah. Some sort of virus, isn't it? A bit unlucky."

"The timing is very unfortunate. And a bit of a coincidence, wouldn't you say?"

"Wait a minute. Have you been talking to Eddie Wonder?"

"I have, yes."

"I might have known. What exactly has he accused me of? Trying to nobble his team? How exactly does he think I managed that?"

I ignored his question because I didn't want to use the word 'poison' in public.

"Did you have anything to do with it?"

"Of course not. How am I supposed to have given them a virus? You can tell Eddie from me, that the Blue Flags are going to win the league, but we'll win it fair and square. On merit, and not because we've sabotaged his team."

***

After my meeting with Teddy Barr, I was walking through Candlefield Market Square, when I spotted a familiar face; it was Eddie Wonder. He stepped inside a small shop. It was one I'd walked past several times, but I'd always assumed it had gone out of business. The faded sign above the door read 'Candle Launderette'.

As I got closer, Eddie re-emerged.

"Hello, Eddie."

"Oh? Hi there."

"Getting your smalls washed?"

"Sorry?" He looked puzzled.

"The launderette? Are you doing the weekly wash?"

"I—err—get my BoundBall kit cleaned there."

"Where is it?"

"Where's what?"

"Your kit?"

"I—err—just took it in."

"I see."

"Anyway, I'd better get going." He started to walk away. "I'm meant to be meeting someone."

"Okay, bye."

How very curious. I was almost positive he hadn't had anything with him when he'd gone into the shop. And why had he been in such a hurry to get away? Surely, I wasn't so scary? I peered through the window of the launderette. There was no sign of life inside—just a row of washing machines—all with their doors wide open.

***

At my request, all of the jewellers except Are Forever had agreed to close for thirty minutes starting at one-forty-five.

"I still don't really understand why we're doing this, Jill." Arnold, the owner of Are Forever, said.

"You'll just have to trust me on this one."

"What do you want us to do?"

"Just carry on as usual. Serve the customers as you would do normally."

"What about you? What will you be doing?"

"I'll be in the back office. If I leave the door ajar, I'll be able to see into the shop. Is that okay?"

"Of course. Is this going to be dangerous?"

"Only for the thief. You, your staff and customers will be perfectly safe, I promise."

He managed a smile, but I could see he was nervous.

It was ten minutes before two. If my hunch was right, things should start to happen within the next few minutes. I took the tin out of my pocket, and headed towards the door.

"What's that?" Arnold said.

"Brown chalk dust." I began to shake the chalk onto the floor around the door. I'd chosen the colour closest to the shade of the wooden floor.

"Is that necessary? What will the customers think?"

"I doubt they'll even notice it."

Once I was in the back again, I fixed my gaze on the area immediately in front of the door.

The doorbell chimed, and an elderly couple walked in

leaving two sets of footprints. I kept watching, and sure enough, a moment later, a third set appeared.

It had taken quite a while for me to develop the spell which I needed. Without Magna Mondale's book and knowledge, I would never have managed it. I'd had to mix and match half a dozen spells to achieve the desired effect. Even now, I wasn't a hundred percent sure it would work. I'd tried it when I was home alone, and it seemed to work, but I'd only know for sure now I was using it in anger.

Just as I'd expected, everyone in the shop appeared to be frozen to the spot. Everyone except for the ugly man helping himself to the tray of rings. And, of course, me.

"Ahem." I coughed. "Excuse me."

He jumped so hard he dropped the rings back onto the counter.

"What? Who? How?" He took a step back.

"Stopwatch, I presume?"

"Who are you? How did you do that?"

"My name is Jill Gooder. I'm—"

"I've heard of you. You're that level seven bird, aren't you?"

"*Bird*?" Not only was he a thief, but a sexist pig as well. "Would you care to explain what you're doing?"

"Me?" He shrugged. "I ain't doing nothing."

"So you admit you are doing something?"

"That's not what I said."

"I think you'll find it is. If you *ain't* doing *nothing*, you must be doing *something*."

"I don't know what you're talking about."

That much was obvious.

"It looked to me like you were stealing jewellery."

"I was just looking at it."

"Does putting it in your pocket help you to see it better?"

He turned, and started to run towards the door. He didn't get far because I cast the 'bind' spell. The rope wrapped around his arms and legs, and sent him crashing to the floor.

"Let me go! You've got no right to hold me here."

"I think you'll find I have."

Just then, Stopwatch's spell must have run its course because the other people in the shop snapped back to life.

"Why are the rings on the counter?" The sales assistant looked confused.

Arnold noticed me standing over Stopwatch. "Jill, what's going on? Who is that?"

"This is your thief."

"How did you catch him? I didn't even see him come into the shop."

"I'll explain all of that later." Or not.

I made a call to Daze to tell her I'd caught Stopwatch. She said she'd meet me in the alleyway at the side of the shop in two minutes.

"Get up." I pulled Stopwatch onto his feet, and helped him to penguin-walk outside.

"Well done, Jill." Daze was out of breath when she appeared in the alleyway. "However did you manage to catch him?"

"I'm right here." He moaned.

"Shut up, you!" Daze pressed her foot hard onto his back. "Speak when you're spoken to."

"I had to concoct a spell that would work the same as Stopwatch's spell. When his spell kicked in, so did mine.

Time stood still for both of us."

"Brilliant. You really should be on level seven."

"All in good time. You'd better get this charmer back to Candlefield before anyone sees us."

Daze took out a pair of what I assumed to be anti-magic shackles, and fastened them to Stopwatch's legs. "That should stop his tricks." Next, she took out her trusty wire mesh net, and threw it over him. "I'd better get back to process him. Thanks again, Jill."

Another case successfully completed. And Leo Riley need never know of my involvement.

Oh bum!

While I'd been in the alleyway with Daze, Arnold must have called the police.

"Jill, are you okay?" Arnold shouted.

"Yeah, I'm fine." Except that I wasn't. Standing next to the counter, staring at me, were two uniformed police officers, and Leo Riley.

"You!" Riley said. "I might have known."

"Hello, Leo."

"What do you think you're doing?"

"Stopping a jewel thief, apparently. The one you weren't interested in."

"Where is he?"

"He got away, I'm afraid."

"Got away? That's just brilliant! Is there no end to your talents?"

"Maybe if you lot had shown a little more interest, I wouldn't have had to get involved."

"I've a good mind to charge you with obstructing the police."

"Go ahead. I can't wait to read the newspaper

headlines."

"How did you know he'd strike here today? Do you have some inside information? If so, you'd better tell me right now."

"Just good old-fashioned detective work. You know, that thing they pay you to do." I turned to Arnold. "You can tell the other shop owners that they won't have any more trouble from that scumbag."

"Thanks, Jill. I for one appreciate what you've done."

"Why are you still here?" Riley growled at me. "Get out of my sight, before I do something I'll regret."

"My pleasure."

Chapter 13

I'd been unfair on Amber and Pearl when I'd criticised them for letting the rooms in Cuppy C without consulting me. They'd actually succeeded in finding two really nice roommates. I'd decided to pay the newcomers a quick visit to see how they were settling in. And, being the generous soul that I am, I'd bought flowers and chocolates as welcome gifts. The twins had gone out and left their assistants in charge, so I went straight upstairs.

"What the—?"

I couldn't believe my eyes.

The doors of the two rooms, which now belonged to Laura and Flora, were wide open. Both rooms looked as though they'd been ransacked. There was stuff all over the floor, the bed and the cupboards. Someone must have broken in. What would the poor girls think so soon after they'd moved in? I hoped they were all right.

"Flora! Laura!"

"Jill, is that you?" The voice came from my room. "We're in here!"

I walked back down the corridor, and pushed open the door. Laura and Flora were sitting on my bed—drinking and smoking!

"What's going on in here?"

"Do you want a drink, Jill?" Flora hiccupped.

"No. I *don't* want a drink."

"Cigarette?"

"No. You can't smoke in here."

"Why not?"

"This is *my* room."

"But we're all roommates now, aren't we?" Flora took a

drag of her cigarette. "Share and share alike?"

"That's not how it works. *Your* rooms are down the corridor. *This* is *my* room."

They shrugged.

"Anyway, what happened to your rooms? It looks like a bomb has dropped in there."

They shrugged again, and then giggled.

"I'm not standing for this. I'm going to tell the twins."

"See if we care." Flora shrugged—shrugging seemed to be her thing.

"Ooh! You brought us chocolates," Laura said. "Oh, look, and flowers."

"No, I haven't." I slammed the door shut, went downstairs, and had a word with one of the assistants.

"Do you know how long Amber and Pearl will be?"

"They said they were going shopping, so they could be some time."

"Would you ask them to call me as soon as they get back?"

"Yeah, okay."

I wasn't going to stand for this. Those two little madams had to go. When the twins had introduced them, they'd been all sweetness and light. Now, they'd turned into the roommates from hell. Smoking, drinking, ransacking the place, and using my room without permission. Just wait until I'd spoken to the twins. Flora and Laura would be out on their backsides before the end of the day.

***

My status as 'the most powerful witch in Candlefield' could be rather embarrassing, but it did have some benefits. I'd found that a lot of people were more willing to talk to me than they might otherwise have been.

Over the previous two days, I'd found out everything I could about the synthetic blood manufacture and distribution operations. One company was responsible for the manufacture — that company was a non-profit organisation that answered directly to the Vampire Council. Their quality control systems were of the highest standard, having been much improved after the earlier incident, which Maxine Jewell had alluded to. It was difficult to see how poison could have been added during the manufacturing stage.

One company, a different one, was responsible for all deliveries. A small army of drivers delivered the blood door-to-door. This immediately struck me as a more vulnerable part of the supply chain. I'd hoped to find that a single driver covered the two areas where David and Bobby lived, but that wasn't the case. The areas were on separate 'runs' covered by different drivers.

I'd managed to get the names and phone numbers of the two delivery drivers in question.

"Hello. Is that Richard Bow?"

"Just a second, I'm hands-free. Let me park the van."

I waited.

"Okay, sorry about that. I can't talk and drive at the same time. Who's speaking?"

"My name's Jill Gooder. I'm a private investigator. Your employer gave me your name."

"Oh? Why?"

"I believe you deliver to the Crowntop area of Candlefield."

"That's right. Every other Wednesday."

"I'm interested in one delivery in particular." I gave him

David Warren's address.

"Hang on while I check my book. I keep a log of every delivery in case there are any problems."

I could hear all sorts of shuffling around. After a couple of minutes, he came back on the line. "Yes, I've got it here."

"Can you confirm you put the parcel in the lockbox?"

The delivery company had told me that all the houses they delivered to had a refrigerated lockbox where the blood could be left if no one was in. The homeowner had a key, and the delivery driver had a master key which fit all the locks on his route.

"Hold on. No, it wasn't. I have a note on this one. Ah, yes. I remember now. The customer met me on the driveway and took it from me. It was raining, and he was wet through."

"You're absolutely sure it was that address?"

"One hundred percent, yes, because it's very rare that I deliver to anyone in person. People are usually out at work, so I mostly put the parcel in the lockbox."

"Okay, Richard, that's most helpful."

I called David Warren who had been discharged from hospital, and was back at home.

"It's Jill Gooder. How are you feeling?"

"Much better than when you came to see me, thanks."

"David, I wanted to ask you about the last batch of synthetic blood that was delivered to you."

"The bad one?"

"Yeah. Did the delivery driver hand the package to you in person?"

"No, I'm always at work when the delivery comes. The

blood was in the lockbox, as usual."

"Are you absolutely sure about that?"

"Positive."

"What about the lockbox itself? Was that okay? Had it been forced open or damaged in any way?"

"No, it was locked as usual; I opened it with my key."

"Okay, David, thanks very much."

I rang the second delivery driver, and asked him to check his records for the delivery to Bobby's address. He told a similar story. He specifically remembered handing the package to the customer who was waiting on the driveway. When I spoke to Bobby, he insisted the blood had been in the lockbox.

It seemed obvious that someone had intercepted the delivery of synthetic blood. They must then have added the poison before placing the package into the lockbox. But who had done it, and how had they gained access to the lockboxes? Who had most to gain from taking out some of the Eagles' key players? There was one obvious candidate.

"Alan, it's Jill. I think I may have found out how your friends were poisoned."

"Do you know who did it?"

"I have my suspicions, but I need something more solid before I can take it to the police. Do you happen to have a photograph of Teddy Barr?"

"So it *was* him?"

"Like I said, I can't be sure yet, so don't say anything to anyone."

"I won't. I have a photo on my phone from the last time

we played the Blue Flags."

"Can you send it to me?"

"Sure, I'll do it now."

Moments later, my phone beeped to confirm the text had been received. I pulled up the attached photo which was of Teddy Barr and Eddie Wonder shaking hands—presumably taken before the game kicked off.

"Thanks, Alan."

"Is there anything I can do, Jill?"

"No, just keep all of this to yourself. If I'm wrong, I'd rather not tarnish an innocent man's reputation, and if I'm right, I'd rather not risk tipping him off."

"I understand, but keep me posted."

"Will do."

***

Just then, I received a phone call from Pearl.

"Jill, I got a message that you wanted us to call you."

"Are you in Cuppy C, now?"

"Yeah."

"Stay put. I need to talk to you both."

"Okay. We'll be in the tea room."

I hurried over to Cuppy C. The twins were enjoying milkshakes and cupcakes.

"Have you two been upstairs yet?"

"No, we've only just got in. We're shattered. Shopping is a tiring business."

"You need to take a look upstairs. Those two witches you let the rooms to, are a nightmare."

"I thought you liked them." Amber had a milk moustache.

"So did I until I saw what they'd done. They've

completely ransacked their own rooms, and when I was here earlier, they were in my room, drinking and smoking."

"Are you sure, Jill?" Pearl looked doubtful. "They both said they were non-smokers."

"And they don't seem the sort to ransack their rooms," Amber said.

"I saw it with my own eyes. I warned them that I'd tell you, but they said they didn't care."

"We'd better see what's going on." Amber led the way.

I followed them. All three doors were closed, and no one answered when Pearl knocked.

"Look inside," I prompted.

"I'm not sure." Pearl hesitated. "We have to respect their privacy."

"Stuff their privacy." I pushed open the door to Flora's room. "See!"

"There's nothing *to* see," Amber said.

"What?" I pushed past her. The room was as tidy as I'd ever seen it. I hurried next door; it was the same. There was no sign of the carnage I'd seen earlier.

"I think you're being a bit too fussy, Jill," Amber said. "These rooms look fine to me."

"But—I—err—they—"

Just then, there were footsteps on the stairs. Moments later, Laura and Flora appeared.

"Hi, there," Laura said—all sweetness and light. "Is there a problem?"

"No." Pearl smiled. "Everything is fine."

"Are you sure?" Flora stepped forward. "We'd rather you said if there's a problem. We wouldn't want to upset anyone."

I glared at them. The two-faced little minxes.

"Everything is okay," Amber said.

The twins started down the stairs. When they were half way down, Laura and Flora both turned to me, and grinned.

***

I was still spitting feathers when I got back to Washbridge.

Mrs V came through to my office. "Are you okay, Jill? You're very red in the cheeks."

"I'm fine, thanks."

"You really should cut back on the caffeine. I don't think it suits you."

"I said I'm fine. Was there something you wanted?"

"Pardon me for caring." She huffed. "There's a woman in the outer office who'd like to see you. Her name is Lacey Ball. She doesn't have an appointment."

"Okay, send her through. And, I'm sorry I snapped at you."

Lacey Ball had short, unkempt brown hair, and looked like she'd got dressed in the dark.

"Hi, how can I help you, Mrs Ball?"

"Call me Lacey, please."

"Okay, Lacey, have a seat. What is it I can do for you, exactly?"

"I didn't know where to turn. I've tried the police, but they don't seem very interested. They won't take it seriously at all."

"Won't take what seriously?"

"I had a phone call two days ago." She hesitated.

"Yes?"

"It was from my sister; we're identical twins."

"Okay."

"She warned me to be careful."

"Careful about what?"

"She didn't say. She just said, 'Lacey, be careful', and then the line went dead."

"Did you try to call her back?"

"The number was withheld."

"Don't you have her number, anyway? Couldn't you have gone around to her house?"

"My sister died in a car crash three years ago."

"Sorry. I thought for a moment there that you said the call was from your sister who died three years ago."

"That is what I said."

"I don't understand."

"Neither do I. It came totally out of the blue."

"Are you sure it was your sister's voice?"

"Of course I'm sure. I know my own sister's voice; I'd know it anywhere."

"I don't want to appear rude, but have you been under a lot of stress lately?"

"I'm not crazy if that's what you mean."

"What did the police say?"

"They said they couldn't help me because their records showed that my sister had died three years ago. That's why I'm here today."

"You say she died in a car crash?"

"Yes, it was a terrible accident. The car went off the road, hit a tree, and caught fire. I don't like to think about it."

"I'm sorry to have brought it up."

"That's okay. I just need someone to help me. Will you?"

"Yes, but I have to tell you this is one of the strangest cases I've come across."

I seemed to be attracting them at the moment.

Chapter 14

I'd popped out of the office to go to the local supermarket to get myself a ginger beer and an Eccles cake. I was just in the mood for a dead fly cake, as we used to call them as kids. It was ages since I'd had one.

As I was walking back to the office, I spotted a familiar figure: a cat. It was Bella. She was racing along the pavement, but wasn't headed towards her apartment block. She was going in the opposite direction. What was she up to? I was curious, so I followed her.

She walked down the side of the building, and began to meow loudly. After two or three minutes, a door opened and I heard someone say, "Bella, come on in."

I rushed down the alleyway, and managed to grab the door before it closed. Inside, an old lady, followed by Bella, was walking down the corridor. She took a key from her pocket, and unlocked the door to one of the apartments. Bella followed her inside.

I gave it a couple of minutes, and then knocked on her door. The old lady answered.

"Hello, yes?"

"I'm sorry to trouble you, but I've just seen Bella go into your apartment."

"She comes here every day, dear. Always around this time. She meows to let me know she's here."

"Do you feed her?"

"Of course. Only the best for Bella, though. She's very picky. I give her salmon occasionally, but she won't touch pink."

I knew the feeling. "How long does she stay here?"

"Usually only for half an hour or so—sometimes an

hour. Although she does occasionally stay overnight, but that's very rare."

"Do you actually know where Bella lives?"

"No idea, dear. I assume it must be somewhere close by. She uses me as a feeding station." The old lady bent down and stroked Bella. "But I don't mind. She's a beautiful cat."

"I'm sorry, I didn't catch your name," I said.

"Mrs Shuman. Not shoe as in a shoe that you put on your foot. Shu as in S-H-U, Shuman."

"Nice to meet you, Mrs Shuman. My name is Jill Gooder. I work in the office building across the road."

"The one with the new sign?"

"That's the one."

"Is it a tanning salon?"

"Not exactly. Look, Mrs Shuman, I know Bella's owners. They're a couple called Bonnie and Clive."

"Didn't they used to rob banks and shoot people?"

"No. It's Clive, not Clyde."

"Oh."

"Anyway, Clive hasn't been well."

"I'm sorry to hear that."

"They're going to have to move, but they can't take Bella with them."

"Oh dear. What will happen to her?"

"That's what I'd like to talk to you about."

***

"Winky!"

"What's up? Couldn't you see I was asleep?"

"I have good news for you, about Bella. She won't be

leaving."

"Have you found somewhere for her?"

"I have."

"You're a superstar. I've always said so."

Words almost failed me.

"An old lady named Mrs Shuman, in the next apartment block down the road, is going to take her in. I've let Bonnie and Clive know. They're thrilled with the arrangement. Bonnie is going to go around to see Mrs Shuman, so they can sort out the details."

"Which floor will she be on?"

"The ground floor."

"Will I be able to see her window from here?"

"I think so."

"That's brilliant. I always knew you'd do it."

"You owe me one, Winky."

"Of course. Your wish is my command."

Hmm? I'd have to remember that.

***

I planned to show the photo of Teddy Barr to Richard Bow, the delivery driver. If he confirmed that the man he'd given the blood to was indeed Teddy Barr, then I'd have enough to take it to Maxine Jewell.

When I rang Richard, he told me that he had a very old-fashioned phone.

"It's one of those you can only make calls on. I can't receive photos or anything like that. I'm sorry."

"Not to worry. Could I meet up with you somewhere, so I can show you the photo face to face?"

"Sure. How about outside the north gate of Candlefield Park?"

"Yeah, that would be fine."

Thirty minutes later, when his van pulled up outside the park gates, I was waiting for him. The van had the name: 'SynBlood' on the side. I knocked on the window.

"Richard?"

"Are you Jill?"

"That's me. Thanks for coming."

"No problem. How can I help? You said something about a photograph?"

I took out my phone and brought up the photo. "Take a look at this. Is that the man who took the blood delivery from you at David Warren's house?"

"Yes, that's him." He touched the screen with his finger.

***

Ever since I'd bumped into Eddie Wonder coming out of the launderette, something had been bugging me about him. He'd seemed so nervous on that day, and yet when I'd first met him, he'd come across as super confident—almost arrogant. With Teddy Barr in the frame for the poisonings, I'd more or less dismissed my concerns about Eddie. But, after my meeting with Richard Bow, I now had good reason to take a closer look at Captain Wonderful.

Something Alan had said came back to me. He'd told me that Eddie had been due to get married; he and his fiancée had even set a date. Then out of the blue, she'd called it off and dumped him. Alan had no idea why.

I'd managed to get her name and phone number from Alan.

"Hello?" A timid voice answered.

"Hi. Is that Amelia Jett?"

"Yes. Speaking."

"Look, you don't know me, but my name is Jill Gooder. I'm a friend of Alan, who plays in the same BoundBall team as Eddie Wonder. I believe you and Eddie were engaged to be married?"

"That's right. Why?"

"Had you heard that a couple of Eagles' players were rushed to hospital recently?"

"No, but then, I've lost touch with the BoundBall scene since Eddie and I broke up."

"That's understandable. I've been asked to see if I can find out what caused their sudden illness. I wondered if I might ask you a few questions about Eddie?"

"What kind of questions? I haven't seen him for a while. He's not ill is he?"

"No, he's fine. I believe you and he were going to be married?"

"Yes, we were." I could hear the sorrow in her voice.

"Why did you call the wedding off?"

"I'd rather not discuss that."

"Was Eddie cheating on you?"

"No, nothing like that. If you must know, it was money problems."

"What kind of money problems?"

"We'd been saving for the wedding for such a long time. We had such great plans. I'd chosen a dress, and picked the hotel where we were going to have the reception, but then—" She hesitated.

"What happened?"

"The money was gone."

"Gone? You mean it was stolen?"

"No. Not stolen. Look, I really don't want to talk about this."

"Amelia, could I just —"

The line was dead.

What did she mean the money had gone? If it hadn't been stolen, and *she* hadn't taken it, that left only Eddie. Had he squandered the wedding money in some way? Was that why she called off the wedding? It certainly sounded like it.

***

"Hello?" I called. "Anyone in?"

The launderette smelled, and not in a good way.

"What do you want?" A werewolf, wearing a hoody, appeared from the back.

"Any chance of a service wash?" I held up my bag.

"Sling your hook."

Customer service was alive and well in Candlefield.

"How much does a service wash cost?"

"I told you. Get lost before I do something you'll regret."

Just then, another man — a wizard — came from out of the back somewhere.

"See you, Tommy," he said to the werewolf as he passed by.

"Yeah. See you, Jim."

I followed Jim out of the shop, and waited until we were out of the market place.

"Excuse me."

"Yeah?"

"I saw you come out of the launderette."

"What about it?"

"Did you get what you wanted?"

"Course I didn't. I never do. I don't know why I keep going back."

"I was thinking of trying it myself."

"Don't! Take it from me. Betting is a mugs game, and once you start, you'll never be able to stop."

"Okay. Thanks for the advice."

***

I was still feeling a little paranoid about my room at Cuppy C. Had those two little witches wrecked it again? Were they in there right now, smoking or drinking? I couldn't rest; I needed to check.

I magicked myself over there, only to find the twins were out again.

"Where are they today?" I asked one of the assistants.

"They've gone to see their accountant."

I couldn't help but wonder if that was true, or if it was code for another shopping expedition. Upstairs, there was no sign of Flora or Laura. My room looked okay, and I couldn't smell alcohol or cigarettes. I didn't look in the other girls' rooms, but I was fairly sure neither of them were in. Satisfied, I made my way back downstairs, and ordered a cupcake and a latte.

From my seat at the window table, I glanced across the road. Sitting by the window in Best Cakes, were two familiar faces. It was Laura and Flora, and they were with Miles and Mindy. Even from this distance, I could see them laughing and joking together. What were they up to? I'd need to keep an eye on those two.

Thankfully, the queue of traffic on the approach to the toll bridge was only a few cars long.

"Hello, Jill." It was Mr Ivers. "I have something for you."

And I had a horrible feeling I knew what it was.

"Look! Your back issues — all twenty-four of them."

"That's very kind of you, but you really shouldn't have bothered."

"It's no trouble. I knew you'd be disappointed to miss out."

Crushed.

"That's seventy-two pounds."

"How much?"

"I realise that's a lot to pay at once, so I've decided to give you a special, one-off discount."

"Thanks."

"We'll call it seventy pounds."

"Seventy? That's still a lot."

"Okay, I'll throw in the price of the toll for that." He passed me the pile of newsletters.

"I don't suppose I could pay in instalments, could I?"

"Sorry, Jill, I really do need the money. As you've probably already gathered, I lost my previous job. I've been out of work for quite some time."

"Seventy pounds?"

"Yes, please, but like I said, that does include the toll."

A car horn beeped. There was now a queue of vehicles behind me.

"Can I pay by card?"

"Sorry, it's cash only."

"Okay." I emptied my purse onto the passenger seat. I had a grand total of seventy-two pounds and fifty-three pence.

"There you go then, Mr Ivers—seventy pounds."

"Thanks, Jill. They should keep you going for a while. There are some really good reviews in there, even if I do say so myself. Would you like me to talk you through the best ones?"

"Not now, thanks. There's quite a queue building up behind me."

"They can wait. If you'd like me to—"

"No! It's okay. I have to get home to make dinner. Maybe another time."

"Okay then. Bye, Jill."

When I got to the house, I carefully filed the newsletters in date order. In. The. Bin.

It was then that I noticed someone in the garden next door—on the opposite side to Mrs Rollo. It was a young woman, probably in her late twenties. She was wearing the shortest shorts I'd ever seen, and a low cut vest top. She had a fantastic figure, beautiful dark hair, and was incredibly attractive.

"Hi," she called. "I'm Megan, Megan Lovemore."

"Hi, Megan. Nice to meet you. Jill Gooder."

"Have you moved in yet?"

"Yes, we've been in for a few days now."

"I'm glad someone is living here again. I don't like living next door to an empty house. I feel so vulnerable because I live here all alone."

"Isn't it a rather big house just for you?"

"I didn't move in by myself. I moved in here with my

husband three years ago, but shortly afterwards, he was killed."

"Oh dear, I'm so sorry to hear that."

"It was a road traffic accident. He was riding a motorbike, and was hit by a combine harvester."

"How terrible."

"It was. The money from the insurance paid off the house, so I could afford to stay. But like I said, I do feel a bit vulnerable."

"I suppose you must."

"It must be nice to have a fella like yours. He's very handsome, isn't he? I hope you don't mind me saying that."

"No, of course not."

"What does he do?"

"He's a policeman."

"Even better. I do love a man in a uniform, don't you?"

"Yeah, but Jack doesn't actually wear a uniform; he's a detective."

"How very exciting. You're so lucky."

"I guess so. What do you do, Megan?"

"I'm a model."

How very surprising.

"I mainly do catalogues, and the occasional catwalk show."

"That must be interesting?" Yawn.

"Not really. I've done it for a long time. I'm looking for something else, but I'm not really sure what. I enjoy gardening, so I was thinking maybe I could start my own business?"

"My brother-in-law has a landscaping business."

"Really? Maybe I should speak to him. Do you think

he'd talk to me?"

"I'm sure Peter would be *more* than happy to talk to you." Kathy probably wouldn't be thrilled about it though.

Just then I heard a car pull up on my drive.

"What do *you* do, Jill?" Megan asked before I could make my excuses.

"Actually, I'm a private investigator."

"How very exciting!"

"Jill? Jill?" I heard Jack calling. He'd obviously gone into the house, and found I wasn't there. Moments later, he appeared at the back door.

"Hiya, Jack!" Megan cooed.

Huh?

"Oh, hi, Megan. How are you?" His eyes were on stalks.

"I'm great, thanks."

"Okay." I stepped in. "We'd better get inside. We've got guests coming over for dinner tonight, haven't we, Jack?"

"Have we?"

I kicked his shin.

"Oh yeah, dinner. Of course."

"Nice to meet you, Megan," I said over my shoulder, as I dragged Jack into the house.

"What's up?" he said, when I pinned him with my death-glare.

"How come you never mentioned Megan before?"

"Didn't I? I thought I had. I met her when I first came to view the house. That day when you couldn't make it."

"No wonder you were so keen to take this house."

"Don't be ridiculous! I didn't think it was important. She seems nice, don't you think?"

"Too nice." Much too nice.

Chapter 15

Jack and I barely spoke over dinner. He continued to insist that he hadn't mentioned Megan Lovemore to me because he didn't think it was important. I still wasn't convinced.

But maybe I was overreacting. Jack and I had got on really well over the last six months while we'd been living together. It had actually been the best six months of my life. Of course, we'd had arguments; which couple didn't? But as soon as he'd admitted he was wrong, everything was okay again.

What? I'm only kidding.

We were both inclined to fly off the handle occasionally. Jack could be hot-tempered, and surprisingly, some people say I can be too. But our relationship was stronger than it had ever been. So why was I worried about a single, attractive, young woman living next door? It was ridiculous. I was being stupid.

We washed the dishes together, each waiting for the other to speak first. A knock at the door eventually broke the silence.

"I suppose I'd better get that?" he said.

I shrugged, but followed him anyway. If it was Megan Lovemore, I'd have something to say about it. It turned out to be a man wearing a trilby.

"I hope you don't mind me calling on you unannounced. My name is Norman Hosey. I live two streets away."

"Hello, Mr Hosey," Jack said. "Is there something I can help you with?"

"I think you'll find that *I'm* the one who can help *you*.

Would it be possible for me to come in for just a couple of minutes?"

Jack glanced at me. I shrugged.

"Yes, I suppose so."

"Jolly good. I won't take up much of your time."

We went through to the living room. Jack and I sat on the sofa together. Mr Hosey sat opposite us.

"I'll get straight to the point. I'm head of the Neighbourhood Watch for Smallwash. I've been in the post now for six years, eight months, two weeks, and three days. During that period, I'm pleased to report that crime levels have fallen consistently. In fact, if you like, I have a graph I can show you."

"No, that's okay." I jumped in. "I'm sure we can take your word for it."

"A not insignificant achievement, I'm sure you'll both agree."

"Very impressive," I said.

Jack nodded. I could tell he wanted to laugh, and if he did, that would set me off. We'd both end up in hysterics.

"I'm sure you'll both agree that neighbourhood watch is the single most important factor in reducing crime."

"Actually," Jack said. "I'm a police officer, and I have to say that I think the police play a big part in that too. And Jill is a private investigator."

Norman Hosey looked a little taken aback. "That's very interesting. Of course, the police play their part. But still, neighbourhood watch does seem to be the single most important factor. As for private investigators, well I'm sure it's an *interesting* job."

Talk about backhanded compliments.

"We're always on the lookout for new members who

can play an active part in neighbourhood watch. I wondered if I could sign you two up?"

I jumped in again before Jack could agree to something that I'd regret later. "Actually, Mr Hosey, the problem is we've only just moved in, and things are still a bit chaotic at the moment. We've got a lot to do, and we both have very demanding jobs."

"I can understand that a policeman would be busy, but a female private detective?"

Condescending or what?

"I have lots of cases. Very long days, and late nights. I'm sorry, but we won't be able to help at the moment. Maybe at some future date?"

"In that case, I'll touch base with you from time to time to see if things have improved, workload-wise."

"That sounds like a good idea."

I thought we'd done, and I was just about to stand up when he continued.

"Jack, tell me. Are you interested in trains?"

"I take one to London, occasionally."

"What about model trains?"

"No, not really."

"How disappointing. It's something of a hobby of mine."

Why didn't that surprise me?

"I have a layout in the loft. In fact, it's probably the biggest in Smallwash, although I do say so myself. I'm always happy to show people if it's something they're interested in. No children though, I'm afraid. They tend to touch."

"Right, thank you. Maybe when we're settled."

Jack was being far too polite and diplomatic. I would

have told him I'd rather eat glass than look at his toy trains.

He still hadn't done. "I also like to visit railway stations, and I have quite a collection of photographs and memorabilia from stations all over the country. You're welcome to see those at the same time."

Oh goody, goody. Maybe I should suggest he talk to Mr Ivers in the toll booth. I had a sneaking suspicion that those two would get on like a house on fire.

"Well, I won't keep you any longer." He stood up. "I'll keep in touch, and maybe when your circumstances change, we can get you involved in neighbourhood watch. But if at any time you would like to see my train set or memorabilia, please do give me a call on this number." He handed us both a business card which had printed on it:

'Norman Hosey - Head of Smallwash Neighbourhood Watch'.

"I'll be only too happy to arrange for you to come over."

We saw Mr Hosey to the door. As soon as he'd gone, we looked at one another and burst out laughing. When we eventually managed to compose ourselves, we kissed.

"It could be worse," I conceded. "I think I'd rather have Megan as a next door neighbour than Mr Hosey."

***

It was Lacey Ball who answered the door when I called at her house. The woman looked like a bag of rags, and had obviously got dressed in the dark again. She offered me tea or coffee, but I declined because I'd dropped into Coffee Triangle en route. It was tambourine day, so the noise levels had been bearable.

We'd no sooner taken a seat in the living room than a

man wearing oversized jogging bottoms came charging into the room.

"What's she doing here?" He pointed at me.

"I've already told you, Joe. Jill is a private investigator. I've asked her to help me with that phone call."

"You mean the one you imagined? It's all nonsense, Lacey." He turned to me. "You're wasting your time here, lady. My wife is delusional; there was no phone call. Her sister died in a car crash three years ago. I'd like you to leave."

"Mr Ball, your wife has asked me to help, and the least I can do is hear her out."

"I said get out!"

"No!" Lacey screamed at her husband. "*You* get out of here, Joe. Leave us alone."

The tension between the two of them was palpable. He huffed and puffed a little, but then left the room, slamming the door closed behind him.

"That's what I'm up against," she said. "It's not just the police who don't believe me. Even my husband doesn't."

"Did the phone call come through on your mobile?"

"No, it was on the landline."

"Can't the police trace it?"

"They probably could, but they're not taking it seriously. As far as they're concerned, my sister is dead."

"Can you tell me exactly what happened three years ago?"

"No one really knows. Mandy was driving home from a night out when the car veered off the road. It hit a tree, and exploded. They checked the car over thoroughly, but couldn't find any mechanical faults."

"Is it possible it could have been suicide?"

"I don't believe it was suicide because Mandy was perfectly happy. If she'd had any problems, she would have told me; we were very close. I've always thought she must have fallen asleep at the wheel; it's the only thing that makes any sense."

"If you did get the phone call, and I have no reason to doubt your word, that means she wasn't killed in the accident, so it must have been someone else in the car."

"I don't know what to think. I want answers, but the police won't do anything. Is it hopeless, or is there anything you can do?"

"Honestly, I don't know. I'm not going to make any rash promises."

"I understand that, but at least if you're looking into it, it gives me some hope. I know everyone thinks I'm crazy, but I know what I heard. It was Mandy on the phone."

As I made my way out, Joe Ball intercepted me. "I want you to drop this!"

"I'm working for your wife. Until she tells me to stop, I intend to carry on doing just that."

He wasn't impressed, but he didn't attempt to stop me when I pushed past him.

***

Eddie Wonder was a few metres ahead of me. Just as I'd expected, he was headed for the launderette. I waited behind a pillar. Five minutes later he came back out, and as he passed by, I stepped out in front of him.

"Jill?"

"Hello, Eddie. You seem to do a lot of laundry."

"Err — Yeah. I have to do all the BoundBall outfits."

"Really? You didn't go in there to place a bet then?"

"I don't know what you mean." I could see the fear in his eyes.

"I think you do. You and I both know that the launderette is just a front for an illegal betting operation. Is that where you've been placing bets on the Eagles to lose?"

"Are you crazy? Why would I bet against my own team?"

"Because from what I hear, you're in an awful lot of debt. You even lost the money that you and Amelia had put aside for the wedding, didn't you? The next bet you placed had to come through for you, didn't it? And the only way you could be certain of winning was to cripple your own team, and then bet against them."

"You're wrong. I would never do anything like that."

"How did you get the keys for the lockboxes? From the changing rooms I assume? It can't have been difficult to make an impression, and then get them cut."

"This is nonsense. You're just making it up."

"I don't need to make it up, Eddie. I've got a witness."

"What do you mean? Who?"

"The driver who delivered the blood. He identified you from a photograph."

Eddie slumped back against the wall.

"What have I done?"

"How much debt are you in, Eddie?"

"Too much. It was my own stupid fault. I should have cut my losses, but I just kept doubling up and doubling up. If I don't get the money soon, I'll be bankrupt and thrown out of house and home. I didn't know what else to do."

"So, to save your skin, you decided to throw the game, and to poison two of your own friends."

"I'm sorry."

"Sorry doesn't really cut it though, does it?"

***

Maxine Jewell wasn't thrilled to hear from me — when was she ever? But once she realised I'd caught the poisoner, her attitude changed. A little.

Eddie was still feeling very sorry for himself as he was being led away.

There was someone else I needed to tell.

"Alan? I thought I should let you know the poisoner has just been arrested."

"Really? Was it Teddy?"

"No. I'm sorry to tell you it was Eddie Wonder."

"Eddie? It can't have been."

"I'm afraid it was. You'll hear all the details in the fullness of time, no doubt, but the Cliff Notes version is that he was in debt big time. He needed the Eagles to lose the big match to clear his debts."

"I can't believe he would poison his own team mates. His friends."

"Desperate men do desperate things sometimes. Anyway, it looks like you're going to be another man short for the game. And you'll have to appoint a new team captain."

"We're really going to struggle now. Anyway, thanks for all your help, Jill. I really do appreciate it."

Chapter 16

The next morning, Jack was making porridge. I was running late, so I just grabbed some cornflakes.

"You'll give yourself indigestion if you eat so fast," he said.

"You sound like my mother. And, get your cup off the table. Why can't you use a coaster? This house is a mess." I sighed. "I don't know when I'm going to find the time to clean. I've got so much work on at the moment."

"Why don't we get a cleaner?" he suggested.

"Are you serious?"

"This house is much bigger than the old place. I work all hours. You're always busy. Neither of us really has the time to clean."

"You don't know who you might get."

"We'd obviously have to vet the applicants, but it would mean we could actually enjoy our leisure time. Otherwise all we're going to do is spend all our free time cleaning the house."

"I'm still not sure. I don't like the idea of somebody else coming into my house."

"Why don't we at least look into it? Let's see what's available, how much it costs, and then maybe interview a few people. If you don't like the look of them, we won't bother."

"Okay, I suppose."

As we were leaving, Megan Lovemore stepped out of her front door.

"Hi, you two." She waved. She was wearing a summer dress, which was fractionally longer than the shorts she'd been wearing the last time I'd seen her. She didn't appear to be wearing makeup, but still looked absolutely stunning.

"Hi, Megan," Jack simpered.

"Morning, Megan." I just about managed a smile.

"I'm glad I bumped into you, Jill. Didn't you say your brother-in-law was a professional gardener?"

"Peter, yeah, that's right. He has his own landscaping business."

"I was being serious the other day when I said it might be something I'd like to do. I want to get out of the modelling game. It's a hard grind."

"It must be." All that walking up and down catwalks, and standing still for photographs. Catty? Who, me?

"Yeah, I've had enough. I'm getting too old. It's a young person's game. Do you think I could possibly meet with your brother-in-law sometime to pick his brains?"

"I guess so. I'm not sure when though."

"You could talk to him at the housewarming," Jack said.

"You're having a housewarming?"

"Yeah. It's on Sunday." Jack nodded. "Peter and his wife, Kathy, will be there. You're more than welcome to join us, isn't she, Jill?"

"More than welcome."

"Thanks. I'll look forward to it. Anyway, I'd better get going. I've got a photo shoot this morning. No rest for the wicked."

"What?" Jack said, after she'd gone. "What did I do?"

"What were you thinking? Why did you invite her to the housewarming?"

"We have to invite the next door neighbours. Anyway, it sounds like she'll be talking to Peter all night, so it's

Kathy who has to worry."

"True. I suppose that could be funny."

***

I couldn't park in my normal spot because Washbridge Council were doing some work on the road. I was forced to drive around until I found another parking space. As I was walking towards the office, I noticed a couple of buses go by. On the side of them was a big advert for Ever A Wool Moment. The whole side of the bus was taken up with the artwork. It was quite impressive, and must have cost a small fortune. A few moments later, I spotted a taxi which had a similar advert on the side of it. Sponsorship of the buses and taxis in Washbridge must have been costing Grandma a small fortune.

A little further up the road, there was a taxi parked in the rank, waiting for customers. I stuck my head through the open passenger window.

"Where do you want to go, love?" The driver said, with his mouth full of chewing gum.

"I'm not actually after a ride. I was just curious. How long have you had this ad on the side of your cab?"

"That thing? It's an embarrassment. I don't have any say in what goes on the side of the cab. That's dealt with by the head office. This one's only been on there for two or three days. But I've already had lots of smart remarks: 'Hey, spotty', and stuff like that."

"Spotty? Sorry, I don't get the connection?"

"It's pretty obvious isn't it? Zittastic? It's zit cream. You know, for spots."

"Zittastic?" I took a couple of steps back, and sure enough, on the side of the taxi, there was now a huge advert featuring an unfortunate young man with acne. He had a big smile on his face, and was holding a tube of Zittastic. Yet, only thirty seconds earlier, I'd seen an advert for Ever on the side. I definitely hadn't imagined it. What was going on?

As I walked away, another taxi drove by in the opposite direction. It too had the same advert for Ever A Wool Moment on it. Grandma was definitely up to something.

When I arrived at the office, I could hear two voices. It was Jules and Mrs V. It was supposed to be Mrs V's day in, and Jules' day off. If Jules was in, I could only assume there was some sort of problem, and that they were arguing. That was all I needed first thing in the morning. I braced myself as I opened the door.

Much to my surprise, they were sitting side by side at Mrs V's desk. Mrs V was knitting, and so was Jules.

"Hello, you two?"

"Morning, Jill." Jules beamed.

"Morning," Mrs V said.

"I didn't expect to find you here today, Jules. Isn't it your day off?"

"Mrs V has offered to teach me to knit, so I said I'd come in. It's going really well, isn't it, Mrs V?"

Mrs V rolled her eyes. "It's going *quite* well, Jules. You're getting there — *slowly*."

I was no expert, but even I could see that whatever Jules was knitting was only fit for the bin. Still, she seemed enthusiastic enough.

"Are you two getting on okay now, then?"

"Oh, yes," Mrs V said. "Now we've reached our agreement, everything's fine. I'll soon have Jules up to speed with the knitting and crocheting."

"Are you going to teach me to crochet as well?" Jules said.

"I don't see why not. Every young lady should know how to knit and crochet. Don't you agree, Jill?"

"Err—yeah, definitely. Anyway—" I needed to change the subject before she asked how my attempts at knitting were coming along. "How's Armi, Mrs V?"

"He's fine. We're going to the Washbridge Yarn Dinner and Dance in three weeks' time. I haven't been for a few years. Apparently, Armi is very light on his feet."

"That's excellent. What about you, Jules? Have you found yourself a new boyfriend?"

She blushed a little. "Gilbert and I are still together, actually."

"I thought you said you were going to dump him."

"I know, but he looked so pathetic. I couldn't bring myself to do it."

"Is he still squeezing his spots?"

"Yes, I'm afraid so."

"Has he tried Zittastic?"

***

I had an appointment with Danny Day, brother of Mandy Day and Lacey Ball. His adoptive parents had tried for years to have a family, but without success. The doctors had assured them that there was no physical reason why they shouldn't be able to have a child, but in the end, frustrated, they'd decided to adopt. Then, as occasionally happens in such cases, his mother had become pregnant with twins when Danny was three years old.

Danny lived with his wife and had a child of his own. Coincidentally, his house was just the other side of the river Wash. He greeted me at the door.

"You must be Jill. Do come in. My wife's taken the youngster out so that we can talk. Would you like a drink? Tea? Coffee?"

"Tea would be nice, thanks."

"Chocolate digestive? They're all we have, I'm afraid."

"No, thanks. Just the tea will be fine."

"I assume this is about Mandy?" He passed me the tea.

"How did you know?"

"I couldn't think of any other reason why you'd want to speak to me."

"Has Lacey been in touch with you, recently?"

"No, we rarely speak these days—maybe two or three times a year, that's all."

"Lacey came to see me at my office. She said that she'd had a phone call from Mandy."

"When? Before the crash? She's never mentioned it to me."

"No. Much more recently. Last week, in fact."

He looked more than a little stunned. "Is this some kind of joke? If so, it isn't funny."

"It isn't a joke, and I have no desire to upset you, but Lacey insists she had a phone call from Mandy, telling her to be careful."

"She'd probably been drinking."

"Possibly, but she seems quite certain."

"But Mandy's dead. You do know that, don't you?"

"Yes, I understand she was killed in a car accident three years ago."

"That's right, so how could it have been Mandy who called her?"

"I don't know, but Lacey is convinced it was her sister. Her husband, Joe, insists that she's delusional, and reckons she must have dreamed the whole thing."

"I've never liked Joe, but as much as I hate to agree with him, I think he's probably right."

"What kind of relationship did you have with Mandy?"

"It wasn't the best. I always had a fantastic relationship with Lacey. As kids, we spent a lot of time together. But for some reason, I never made the same bond with Mandy. It's not like we fought; we just had very little in common. Lacey and I were probably closer than she and Mandy ever were, which is unusual given that they were twins."

"You say that you and Lacey were very close, but earlier you mentioned you only see each other two or three times a year now. Why is that?"

"It really saddens me. It all changed after Mandy died. It hit both of us hard, but Lacey never really recovered. As the months went by, we saw less and less of one another. She rarely called me, and when I tried to call her, I'd mostly get voicemail. She never returned my calls. I got the feeling that she didn't want to see me. Maybe seeing me reminded her too much of Mandy. I don't know."

"What about friends? Did Mandy have any close friends who I could speak to?"

"She didn't have many friends at all. Not compared to Lacey, at least. The only two I can think of off-hand are Judy Brown and Bev Timpson."

"Do you have contact details for them?"

"I'm sure I do, somewhere."

***

I'd managed to arrange an appointment with the pathologist who'd dealt with Mandy Day's autopsy. Aaron West was a gangling man who never cracked a smile. But then, there probably wasn't much to laugh about in his job. My father had first introduced me to Aaron, and over the years, we'd established some kind of rapport.

"What was the name again, Jill?"

"Mandy Day." I'd already given him the date of her death.

"Jeremy Day, Katherine Day, ah, here it is." He clicked the mouse. "Mandy Day, now let me see." He studied the screen for a few minutes. "Yes, as you say, a road traffic accident. The body was very badly burned. She was identified by a DNA match with her twin sister. Her sister also identified the jewellery that Mandy had been wearing."

"Thank you very much, Aaron. I appreciate your help."

I'd hoped that the identification process might have left room for some doubt, but DNA was about as conclusive as it got. It was looking increasingly likely that Lacey *had* imagined the whole thing.

There was still one thing bugging me though, and that was Lacey's husband, Joe. He was almost certainly right — his wife must have imagined the phone call. But that didn't explain his venom. It wasn't just that he'd been dismissive; he'd been downright aggressive, and had seemed almost scared at the prospect of my investigation.

I had a nagging suspicion that he had something to

hide. I had no other leads, so what harm could it do to take a closer look at him?

Chapter 17

Aunt Lucy poured me a cup of raspberry tea; it was delicious. She'd also made raspberry cupcakes which were absolutely yumcious.

"Hmm these are lovely, Aunt Lucy."

"It's been a while since I've done any baking, what with all of the weddings and everything."

I knew what she meant. The last twelve months had been all weddings. First Aunt Lucy's, and then the twins' double wedding. I'd never worn so much pink.

"How is Lester, anyway? I haven't seen him for a while."

"He's fine. Very busy though."

"The reason I came over this morning is to let you know we're having a housewarming party."

"You didn't sound very keen on the idea the last time we spoke."

"I'm still not, but there's no way to avoid it. Jack's determined to have one, and it's going to be this Sunday. He's asked if my birth family will come over. What do you think?"

"We'd all love to be there, but is it going to be a problem for you?"

"I don't know; I hope not. It depends whether he asks about us paying you a return visit."

"Don't worry about that, Jill."

"I can't help it. I don't want to keep using the 'forget' spell on him."

"I understand. The best thing to do is stick with the same story we told Kathy — that we live in Malten."

"I just worry that one day they're going to want to come

to Malten to see you."

"That isn't a problem. If and when that happens, we'll be able to sort something out. A bit of magic can resolve most things."

"Will you and Lester both come on Sunday?"

"Yes, we'll be there."

"What about the twins?"

"Just try stopping them."

"And Alan and William?"

"The twins will make sure they come, whether they want to or not."

"What do you think I should do about Grandma?"

"You don't have a choice, Jill. If you don't ask her, she'll make your life a misery when she eventually finds out."

"Ahem." Someone coughed.

We both turned around, and there she stood.

"It's okay. You two just carry on talking about me as though I'm not here."

"You *weren't* here, Mother," Aunt Lucy said. "Not when we started this conversation."

"It's a good thing I happened to pop in then, isn't it?"

"'*Happened to pop in*'? You were eavesdropping, more like."

"So, what's this thing that I may or may not be invited to?"

"We're having a housewarming party this Sunday."

"You and that human of yours?"

"His name is Jack."

"Oh yes. Jack and Jill!" She laughed.

"Like I said, we're having a housewarming at the new house on Sunday, and you're welcome to come. Unless, of course, you're busy."

"No, I'm not busy at all. Sunday is free at the moment; you're in luck."

So why didn't I feel lucky?

"Grandma, look, we have to be careful. I don't want Jack to find out that I'm a witch."

"What do you take me for? Do you think I'm going to walk in, and say, '*oh by the way did you know that Jill's a witch*'?"

"I know you won't do that, but when you've had a few drinks—"

"Excuse me, young lady. Are you trying to say I can't hold my drink?"

"You didn't hold it very well that night you went out with Mrs V."

"That was an exception."

"Anyway, Grandma, you mustn't mention Candlefield."

"I'm not an idiot. Of course I won't. So what story have you come up with?"

"I thought we could say that we all live in Malten, Mother," Aunt Lucy said.

"Malten? Where's that?"

"It's about forty miles from Washbridge."

"Okay. I'll try to remember. Maltfleet it is."

"Not Maltfleet, Malten!"

"That's what I said. I'll see you all on Sunday, then."

And with that Grandma disappeared.

There was a knock at the door; Aunt Lucy answered it.

"Jill, it's someone to see you."

"Me? Why would someone come to see me here?"

It was a female werewolf, very tall, elegant and more

than a little scary.

"Jill Gooder?"

"Yeah, that's me."

"I hope you don't mind me calling on you here." She turned to Aunt Lucy. "Is it possible for me to have a few words with Jill, in private?"

Aunt Lucy nodded. "Of course, no problem, I'll go and make a start on the ironing."

"I'm Tabitha Hathaway, the acting chair of the Combined Sup Council."

"Nice to meet you." I'd heard of the Combined Sup Council; it had representatives on it from all the different paranormal creatures that lived in Candlefield. I hadn't had any direct contact with them until now.

"How can I help you, Miss Hathaway?"

"Call me Tabitha, please. I'm here on behalf of the council to offer you a position on the board."

"The board of the Combined Sup Council? Why me?"

"Oh please, no false modesty. It's well known that you are now acknowledged as the most powerful witch in Candlefield."

"But I'm still only level four."

"By choice, from what I hear. And besides, levels are irrelevant in this situation. As I said, the board feels that your input would be invaluable."

"What would it require of me exactly?"

"It won't be a big sink on your time. The Combined Sup Council is more of a figurehead body. Ours is more of a guiding hand. We tend to look at the bigger picture, and offer advice where we feel it is necessary."

"So you don't have any power as such?"

"It depends on what you call *power*. It's very rare that

our advice is ignored. What do you say? Will you join us?"

"I don't know what to say. This has come totally out of the blue. I'm obviously flattered to be asked, but I'm not sure that I have the necessary qualifications."

"Of course you do."

"I'd like to think about it for a while if I may; it's a big step to take."

"Of course. No need to rush into your decision. Here's my number." She passed me a card. "Give me a call any time. We'd love to have you on board."

***

I had to find out if my suspicions about Joe Ball were correct. To do that, I'd need to shake things up a little.

I parked my car a little way up the road from where he and Lacey lived, and then walked to the small park, which was directly opposite their house. From a bench beneath an overhanging tree, I had a perfect view of their front door. Now, all I had to do was wait. At least the weather was on my side for once.

After about an hour, I spotted Lacey coming out of the house. I had my fingers crossed that Joe wouldn't be with her. My luck was in. She got into the car alone, and drove away. I gave it a few minutes, and then walked over to the house.

"What do you want?" Joe was stony-faced.

"Could I see Lacey, please?"

"She isn't here. I've already told you that you're wasting your time with this nonsense."

"Possibly not."

"What do you mean by that?"

"I'm sorry, but Lacey is my client. I can only discuss the case with her."

"Discuss what exactly? You can't have found anything. There's nothing to find."

"Like I said, I can't talk to you about it. Perhaps you'd tell Lacey that I called, and that I've uncovered new information that I'd like to discuss with her."

"She's not interested. And don't think we're going to pay you."

He slammed the door in my face. That was just the reaction I'd hoped for.

Just in case he was watching me, I set off down the street, but then after a couple of minutes, doubled back to the park. I didn't have long to wait. Five minutes later, Joe emerged and jumped into his car. I sprinted to mine and began to follow him. I could tell by the way he was driving that he was still irate. Just as I'd hoped, I'd succeeded in getting his back up.

He parked on the road close to Washbridge Park. Fortunately, there were plenty of free spaces, so I was able to park further down the road without him noticing. I followed him into the park; he was obviously a man on a mission. He made his way over to the small café, which was close to the children's play area. He didn't bother to buy a drink or anything to eat. Instead, he joined a young woman who was sitting alone at a table. I kept my distance, and hid behind a tree from where I could watch them. They were very animated. He was waving his arms about; she was shaking her head. I needed to hear what was being said, so I used the 'listen' spell.

"You can't do this, Joe!" The woman was close to tears.

"I'm sorry."

"You said you were going to leave her at the end of the month. Why did you lie to me?"

"I didn't. It's just that Lacey and me are going to give it another go."

"You said you couldn't bear to be in the same room as that woman!"

"Things change. I'm sorry." He stood up, and walked away.

This time I didn't follow him. Instead, I made my way over to the woman.

"Are you all right? I couldn't help but notice you were crying."

"I'm okay." She took a tissue from her pocket, and wiped her eyes.

"Are you sure? Is there anything I can do to help? Did that man do something to upset you?"

"No, it's okay. I'm fine. It's my own stupid fault. I should have known better than to get involved with a married man. They're all the same. He said he was going to leave his wife, but now he's called it off." The woman stood up. "I don't know why I'm telling *you* all of this. Sorry. I have to go."

So, Joe Ball had been having an affair, and had promised to leave Lacey at the end of the month. Why the sudden change of heart? Why call it off immediately after my visit?

***

When I'd suggested meeting at lunchtime for a drink, Kathy had insisted that we go to Bar Piranha. I hadn't been in there for some time. When it first opened, as Bar Fish, the place had been delightful. It had been full of beautiful, tropical fish, and even though it could feel a bit creepy at times with all those eyes on you, it had been quite relaxing. When the original owner, Stuart Steele, had been sent to prison for the murder of Starr Fish, the business had gone into administration. Its new owners had rebranded it to Bar Piranha. They'd got rid of the tropical fish, and replaced them with piranhas. They totally freaked me out. The fish were in tanks that ran under your feet, along the walls and even behind the bar. Although I knew the glass was too thick for them to be able to get out, I still found them really scary. Thankfully, they were only fed when the bar was closed. I had no desire to see them ripping some animal carcass to pieces. Yuk!

We took a seat near to the window.

"Why did we have to come here, Kathy? Look at those horrible things. Look at their teeth!"

"I think they're cute."

"Cute? Piranhas aren't cute. If you put your hand in there, they'd tear it to the bone within seconds."

"I still think they're cute. So, how's everything going with the party preparations?"

"Okay, I guess."

"You haven't managed to talk Jack out of it, then?" She laughed.

"Why would I? I'm looking forward to it."

"Liar. You hate parties."

"No, I don't."

"You've never liked them. When we were kids, and Mum and Dad gave us the option of a party or a day out on our birthday; you always chose the day out."

"I like to visit places."

"I always chose the party," Kathy said. "Parties are fun."

"That's a matter of opinion."

"See, that's what I mean; you're a killjoy. Who else is going to be there?"

"Some of Jack's friends from Washbridge police station, Mrs V and Jules, some of the neighbours, and my birth family."

"Aunt Lucy and the twins?"

"Yep."

"Your grandmother?"

"Yep."

"Can the kids come?"

"Some of Jack's friends will be bringing their kids, so I can hardly turn yours away."

"How will you cope? Your poor new house and all that lovely furniture."

"Don't. It makes me want to cry every time I think about it. Let's talk about something else. What's going on with all the advertising Grandma's doing? I've seen loads of buses and taxis with Ever A Wool Moment on the side."

"They've only appeared in the last few days; there are dozens of them. It must be costing her a small fortune. I've tried to ask her about it, but she's being really cagey. She said she didn't want to talk about it."

Chapter 18

Although I liked the idea of someone doing the cleaning, I *didn't* like the idea of them having to come into my house to do it. In the end though, I'd agreed that we'd at least look for a cleaner, and see what we came up with. We'd checked the local listings, and found three or four possible candidates. The first one was coming in that morning. Jack and I were going to talk to her together.

But then Jack's boss called. He had to go into work straightaway—no questions asked.

"What about the cleaner? We're meant to be interviewing her in ten minutes."

"I'm sorry, Jill. You heard the phone call; I don't have any choice."

"This is getting to be a habit. Are you sure you aren't paying somebody to make these calls just to get you out of this stuff?"

He laughed.

"I wouldn't put anything past you."

"You're perfectly capable of deciding whether this woman will be any good or not. If you're happy with her, then set her on. Look, I've got to go. See you later, bye."

Great! That was the only drawback of working for myself. I could hardly pretend that someone had phoned to ask *me* to go in early. I didn't know anything about this woman, only that she worked under the name of Mopp Cleaning Services. Hopefully her cleaning was better than her spelling: Mop with two 'p's? Dearie me!

Jack had only been gone a few minutes when there was a knock at the door. It was so loud I thought the door was about to cave in.

"Just a minute! I'm coming!"

There was another knock—even louder this time. How impatient!

"Is this the Gooder residence?"

"Yeah, I'm Jill Gooder."

"I'm Miriam Mopp. I believe you're expecting me."

"Mopp's your name?"

"Of course it's my name. Why else would I call the company Mopp Cleaning Services?"

"Oh? I thought that was mop as in the kind you clean the floor with."

"No, dear, that would be mop, my name is Mopp with two 'p's, M-O-P-P."

"Right, sorry for the confusion."

"Can I come in? It's rather chilly out here."

"Yes, of course. Come in. Let me take your coat, Mrs Mopp."

Mrs Mopp? How did I not laugh?

"Let's go through into the living room. Please have a seat over there."

"Right then, we'd better start the interview," Mrs Mopp said.

"Quite right, we should. Can I—"

But before I could get the words out, she jumped right in. "Have you had a cleaner before?"

"No."

"Oh dear." She tutted and gave me a disapproving look. "I do hate working for newbies. Their expectations are often unrealistic. Still I'm here now. Do you have any children?"

"No."

"Well, that's a plus at least. Pets?"

"No pets either."

"How often would you want someone to come in and clean?"

"We hadn't really thought—"

"For a house this size, with just the two of you, no children and no pets, once a week is more than enough. I'll need to take a proper look around, but I would guess it will require three hours, maybe only two and a half."

"Right, yeah okay, I was just going to ask—"

"If I'm going to do this, it will have to be on Wednesdays at eight o'clock in the morning."

"That's a little early—"

"I'm afraid that's the only spot I have available. Take it or leave it."

"What would it cost?"

"Twenty pounds an hour plus materials."

"Materials? I have my own cleaning—"

"Sorry, but a professional has to have the right equipment and materials. I insist on providing my own."

"Oh. I see."

"Right, well I think that's probably everything. You can show me around the house now, and I can make a start next Wednesday."

"*Next* Wednesday?"

"Yes. At eight o'clock sharp. And please make sure you're both dressed by then."

"Right. Okay. Will do."

Ten minutes after she left, I was still trying to figure out what had happened. Who exactly had interviewed who?

***

Danny Day had given me the names of two of Mandy's

friends. If she *was* still alive, then maybe she'd been in contact with one of them. And even if she hadn't, they might still be able to throw some light on Mandy's death. Had it been suicide?

Judy Brown had been surprised that someone wanted to talk to her about Mandy after all that time, but she readily agreed to see me.

"Come in. I'm Judy, nice to meet you. How is Danny? I haven't seen him since Mandy's funeral."

"He seems fine. He told me that you were one of Mandy's best friends."

"I suppose I was, but then Mandy didn't have many. She was a bit of a loner. So different from her sister."

"I realise this may sound like a strange question, but have you heard from Mandy since the funeral?"

"Huh? You're right. That is a weird question. Do you mean like a séance or something?"

"No. I meant a phone call."

"She's dead. How could I have had a phone call from her?"

"It's just that her sister says Mandy contacted her by phone recently."

"That's ridiculous. Is Lacey okay?"

"I think so. Did you see Mandy in the days leading up to the car crash?"

"Yes, we were in regular contact. We used to go for coffee at least once a week. Sometimes we'd go swimming together."

"How did she seem? Could she have been depressed? There's been some suggestion that the crash might have been suicide."

"I don't believe that for one moment. Mandy hadn't

always been happy, but right then, just before her death, she was the happiest she'd ever been. She'd started seeing someone."

"A man, you mean?"

"Yeah, she was really excited about it."

"Her brother didn't mention a boyfriend. What was his name? Do you know where I can contact him?"

"That's the thing. Mandy wouldn't say who it was. She was very secretive about it. I never did understand why."

***

Mandy Day's other friend, who Danny had mentioned, was a woman called Beverly Timpson. She lived outside of Washbridge — ten miles to the west.

"You must be Jill; come on in. Call me Bev; everyone does. It's quite a while since I heard Mandy's name. Your call took me by surprise."

"I hope I didn't upset you."

"A little maybe, but it's all a long time ago now."

"I've just been to see Judy Brown."

"The three of us were quite close at one time, but after Mandy died, I lost touch with Judy. How is she keeping?"

"She seems fine. Look, I'll get straight to the point. I'd like to ask you the same question that I asked Judy. I know this is going to sound really strange, but have you heard from Mandy recently?"

She looked at me nonplussed. "I don't understand."

"Since the funeral."

"Is this some sort of sick joke?"

"No, nothing like that. Look, I'm sorry if I've upset you, but the reason I'm here, is that Mandy's twin sister, Lacey, contacted me. She received a phone call the other day warning her to be careful. According to her, the person who called was Mandy."

"But that's impossible. Mandy's dead. She died in a horrible car crash."

"All the evidence suggests that's true, and yet Lacey is convinced that it was her sister she spoke to."

"She must have been mistaken."

"Quite possibly, but I need to cover all the bases. So, I take it that you've never seen or heard from Mandy since the funeral?"

"No. Definitely not."

"What was Mandy like? Were she and her sister alike?"

"I'd known Mandy and Lacey since we were kids. They were very different; it was hard to believe they were twins. Lacey was outgoing, and had a large circle of friends. Mandy was much quieter; kind of shy and insecure. She had very few friends. It was just me, Judy, and maybe a couple of others. Mandy wasn't obsessed with her looks like Lacey. I mean, Lacey used to spend a small fortune just on having her nails done."

"Were you aware of any problems that Mandy was having just prior to her death?"

"No. I know there was some suggestion the crash may have been suicide, but I don't believe that. She may not have been as happy-go-lucky as Lacey, but she would never have taken her own life. In fact, just before her death, she seemed happier than I'd seen her for a long time."

"Judy said a similar thing. She thought Mandy was seeing a man, but she didn't know who."

"I'd noticed a change in Mandy too. She'd hinted that

she was with someone, but she wouldn't say who he was, or tell me anything about him. I wasn't sure whether to believe her or not. She could be a bit of a dreamer sometimes."

***

I popped into Ever A Wool Moment because I wanted to speak to Grandma about the approach I'd had from the Combined Sup Council. When I opened the door to the back office, she jumped.

"Were you asleep, Grandma?"

"Of course not."

She obviously had been.

"Do you have a moment?"

"Not really, but I suppose now you're here, you'd better grab a seat. What can I do for you, young lady?"

"The other day when I was at Aunt Lucy's, I had a visit from Tabitha Hathaway."

"The acting chair of the Combined Sup Council?"

"Yeah, that's her."

"What did she want with you?"

"She's invited me to join the board."

"Has she now? How very interesting. Witches have always been underrepresented on the Combined Sup Council. Are you going to accept the offer?"

"I don't know. That's why I came to see you—to ask your advice."

"Always a wise move."

"What do they do exactly?" I asked.

"That's a very good question. They don't have any real power. They don't actually make laws, but they do have a lot of influence. It's the only body that combines all the different sup types. It would be a foolish person who ignored their wishes. To be honest though, they haven't really come up with very much of interest in recent years. They need some new blood on there. I think you should do it, Jill."

"You do? But, I don't feel I'm qualified."

"You can't keep hiding behind that excuse. You've already turned down promotion to level seven. Don't make matters worse by turning this offer down as well."

"Okay. I'll definitely give it serious consideration. Oh, and there's something else I wanted to mention to you, Grandma, while I've got you here."

"Yes, what is it now? I am rather busy."

"I haven't seen Ma Chivers for over a year."

"Surely you're not complaining about that? Good gracious woman, I would have thought that was a reason to celebrate."

"I don't particularly *want* to see her, but it's strange that she's disappeared. And not just her. There's Alicia, her partner in crime—I haven't seen her for over a year either. Or Cyril, Alicia's sidekick."

"Good riddance to all of them, that's what I say."

"But where do you think they've gone?"

"Between you and me, quite a few wicked witches have dropped out of sight. I noticed it a while back, and a couple of other level six witches have mentioned it to me. They've probably moved to the human world to lie low for a while."

"Maybe so. It's just a little disconcerting. Also, the last time I saw Ma Chivers she said something strange. She said that TDO had never really been her boss; that he was just a pretender to the throne. She said The Phoenix was the one I should be worried about. Do you know who that is?"

"The Phoenix? No. I've never heard of him. I think she was just trying to scare you. She can't have been very happy to see TDO defeated in that way. So rather than lose face, she probably conjured up some cock-and-bull story about this Phoenix character. I should just ignore it. Let's hope Ma Chivers and her cohorts stay away. Good riddance, that's what I say."

Chapter 19

The next morning, Jack had just left for work. I was finishing off the last of my Rice Krispies when there was a knock at the door. He'd probably forgotten something again. But if so, why hadn't he used his key to get back in? Maybe he'd left his keys in the house. It wouldn't have been the first time. I opened the door fully expecting to see Jack, but it wasn't him.

The man at my door was a wizard.

"Can I help you?"

"You're Jill Gooder, aren't you? I've been waiting until you were alone to come over."

That sounded a bit suspicious, and a whole lot of creepy.

He must have seen my expression because he continued. "I guess that sounds rather bad. It wasn't meant to come out that way. I should introduce myself. I'm Blake. Blake Lister."

"You're a wizard, aren't you?"

"Yeah. I live just across the road."

"I didn't realise there were any other sups around here."

"There aren't many of us, to be honest. I think it's just me, you, and a vampire who lives a few streets away. I wondered if I could have a quick word—if you're not too busy."

"I have to leave for work soon."

"This will only take a minute."

"Okay, come in. Would you like a cup of tea?"

"No, thanks. I don't want to hold you up."

"How long have you lived in Smallwash, Blake?"

"Just over four years. I was really pleased to see another sup move in across the road. It can feel a bit isolated out here."

"Do you go back to Candlefield often?"

"Not as often as I'd like. I've still got family over there. It's not easy though."

"Tell me about it. I'm in the same position. I've got family in Candlefield too. So far, Jack's only met my grandmother. I had no idea just how difficult it would be. Before Jack and me moved in together, it wasn't so bad. But living with somebody full-time? That's a different kettle of fish altogether. I assume you're married to a human woman?"

"That's right. Jennifer. Jen."

"We're having a housewarming on Sunday. If you and Jen are not doing anything, you're welcome to come over."

"That's great. I'm sure she'll be up for that."

"How do you manage to hide the fact that you're a wizard from your wife? Have you had any close calls?"

"Not recently. I don't use magic around Jen at all. Even though there are times when I'd like to. Like when I'm mowing the lawn or doing the dishes."

"Don't mention dishes."

"Why, what happened?"

"It was so stupid. The other day I was really tired, and we had a sink full of washing up. Jack was going bowling, and he'd left me to it. He'd only just gone out the door, when I used a spell on the dishes. It turned out he'd forgotten his keys, and he walked back in."

"Oh dear. What happened?"

"I had no choice. I had to use the 'forget' spell on him.

The biggest problem though, is when he asks about my birth family. I was adopted and raised by humans, and I didn't know I was a witch until quite recently."

"Yeah, I've heard a lot about you. Aren't you the witch who turned down the opportunity to go to level seven?"

"That's me. Anyway, like I said, I grew up in Washbridge, and only recently found out about my other family. Jack doesn't understand why he can't visit them. I don't know what to tell him. I have to keep using the 'forget' spell, but I don't like doing it."

"I'm the same. I don't like using magic on Jen. It just doesn't seem right."

"My birth family are coming over here for the housewarming, so that could be interesting. "

"I'll keep my fingers crossed for you. Look, I'd better go. I just wanted to say hello."

"Nice to meet you, Blake. We'll see you both on Sunday, I hope."

"Yeah. We'll be there."

***

My phone rang.

"Jill? It's Lacey Ball."

"Hi, Lacey. I'd planned on giving you a call later to bring you up to speed."

"There's no need. I'd like you to stop the investigation. Obviously I'll pay you for the time you've spent on it up until now."

"But why? I think I might actually be making some progress."

"Joe was right. I'm sure it was all in my imagination.

I've been under a lot of stress. I must have dreamed the phone call. I've been having a lot of nightmares recently."

"You haven't been pressured into this change of heart, have you? Would you like to meet somewhere away from your house to talk about this?"

"No. No one has pressured me. I've just come to my senses. We buried Mandy three years ago. I must have imagined the phone call."

"But, Lacey—"

"Just send me your bill would you, please?"

And with that, she hung up.

Why the sudden change of heart? I couldn't help but feel it was related to Joe Ball's liaison with the woman in the park. I'd obviously spooked him, but why would that have caused him to call off his affair? And more importantly, why was Lacey trying to shut down the investigation?

If I'd had any sense, I would have left it at that. But I didn't, so that was never going to happen. I needed to find out exactly what the police knew about the Lacey Ball case. According to her, she'd told the police that she'd had a phone call from her sister, but that they hadn't been interested.

Even though I wasn't Washbridge Police's biggest fan, I doubted they would have simply dismissed her call for help out of hand. I needed to find out what, if anything, they'd done.

Getting in and out of the police station was child's play for me now. I had any number of spells that could get me inside: I could use the 'shrink' spell, or the 'doppelganger' spell, or even the 'invisibility' spell. This time, I opted for invisibility, and made my way to what had once been Jack's office. It didn't take me long to find the records I was looking for. I found a file on Mandy Day which was from three years earlier. It concerned the car crash, and concluded that it had been an accident, which had probably been caused by the driver falling asleep at the wheel. I continued to look for other records held under either Mandy's or Lacey's name, but there was nothing at all. There was no record of Lacey's recent request for help, which I found very strange. The one place that would tell me for sure was the telephone log. The police recorded every incoming call that they received.

I logged onto the system, using the password I'd set up for myself when Jack was still working there. After I'd done that, it was a trivial matter for me to get into the phone log, and even easier to sort it by name. There was no record of a recent telephone call from Lacey Ball.

What did that mean? It seemed to suggest that Lacey had never even reported the call to the police. So why had she told me that she had? It didn't make any sense.

***

I was on my way back into the office when I literally bumped into two enormous young men. These guys had muscles — everywhere.

"Sorry," I said, trying to get out of the way.

"Our fault." They stepped aside.

"Do you have the office at the top of the stairs?" One of them asked.

"Yeah, that's me. I'm Jill Gooder. Were you on your way to see me?"

"No. We're going to be taking over the rest of the building."

"You're I-Sweat?"

"That's us. How did you know?"

"I bumped into Zac, the landlord, the other day. He said that you'd signed the lease."

"I'm George and this is Brent."

We shook hands. My hand felt small and pathetic in theirs.

"When are you planning to open?"

"We've got a fair number of structural alterations to complete. Then we've got to fit it all out. It'll be a while yet. You'll have to come along and give it a try when we're open."

"I might do that. Where have you been based until now?"

"We had a small gym on the other side of town, but we've outgrown it. The membership has increased, and we need something better — something more modern. We've been looking for somewhere for ages. Finding the right building in the right part of Washbridge, has proven to be much more difficult than we thought. To be honest, when we saw the 'To Let' sign, we assumed it was for the whole building. We hadn't appreciated that someone else was in here. I don't suppose we could persuade you to move out, could we? We could really do with your office too, so that we have the whole building."

Oh, no. Deja vu.

"I'm afraid not. I've been here for quite a while, and I've no plans to move."

"What is it that you do exactly?" Brent said. "Is it a tanning salon or something?"

After I'd finished talking to the two I-Sweat guys, I made my way upstairs into the outer office. Mrs V was behind the desk. There were two young women sitting in the chairs opposite her.

"Are these two young ladies here to see me, Mrs V?"

"They said that they're here for the quick tan."

"Sorry, ladies. I think you must have the wrong address."

"Aren't you a tanning salon, then?" the one wearing purple lipstick said.

"No, we're not."

"But you've got an orange and white sign."

"Didn't you see the letters after my name? Jill Gooder P.I."

"We thought that was like some kind of tanning qualification."

"I'm a private investigator."

"So you don't do tans, then?"

"No, sorry. But there is going to be a health club opening next door soon. They might have sunbeds."

"Oh, okay. We'll probably give them a try when they're open. Thanks."

"Why didn't you just tell them we didn't do tanning, Mrs V?" I asked, after they'd left.

"I would have, but I'd already seen the men delivering the sunbed, so I thought maybe you'd decided to branch out."

"What sun bed?"

"Two men took it through to your office. I didn't know what to think."

That made two of us.

Winky was lying on the sunbed in the middle of my office. He was wearing goggles.

"Hey! You!"

"What?"

"What is this doing here, Winky?"

"Giving me a tan. What do you think? Do I look good?"

"You're a cat. Cats don't have tans."

"Only because they don't have easy access to sunbeds."

"What's this thing doing in here anyway? I hope you haven't paid for it on my credit card."

"No, of course not."

"Or debit card?"

"No. What do you think I am?"

"How did you get it here, then?"

"A guy rang up. He'd driven past, seen the sign, and thought it was a tanning salon. He's in the business of renting and selling sunbeds. He left a message on your answerphone to see if he could interest you in one. I called him back to say that we'd take one on a free trial, and see what we thought of it."

"If he was a human, how did you even speak to him?"

"Haven't you heard of text-to-voice?"

"Heard of what?"

Chapter 20

The next morning when I left the house, Mrs Rollo was already out in the garden.

"Morning, Mrs Rollo."

"Hello there, Jill. How are you settling in? I saw Jack leave earlier."

"I think we're getting there. By the way, I've been trying to catch you. We're having a housewarming on Sunday. I realise it's short notice, but we'd love you to come."

"That would be lovely. I do enjoy a party. I tell you what. I'm not doing much today, so I could do the catering for you. It wouldn't cost you anything apart from the ingredients."

I'd already seen the results of Mrs Rollo's baking. It was an absolute disaster. There was no way I could let her cater for the party.

"That's very kind of you, Mrs Rollo, but actually the catering has already been organised."

She looked crestfallen. "Maybe I could bake a cake for you? You can never have too much cake, can you?"

"That's true." At least, under normal circumstances.

"Is there any particular kind you like?"

Preferably one that actually resembles a cake. "Something simple. Nothing too complicated."

"Do you like Victoria Sponge?"

"Yes, I am rather partial to it."

"Then that's what I'll do. I'll get on with it today, and let you have it tomorrow. What time do you want me to come over on Sunday?"

"Around four o'clock."

"Lovely. I'll bring the cake over tomorrow, and I'll be

there in my glad rags on Sunday. Thanks, Jill. You've made my day."

***

Jules was behind her desk when I walked into the office, but I might as well have been invisible for all the notice she took of me. She seemed to be in a world of her own.

"Jules? Are you okay?"

She snapped out of it. "Oh, sorry, Jill. I didn't see you come in. I was miles away."

"Yeah. I could see that. Are you sure you're okay?"

"I'm fine. It's just that a few minutes ago, before you came in, we had a visitor. One of the guys from the new place next door, you know — the gym —"

"I-Sweat?"

"Yeah. I think he said his name was Brent."

"I've already met him. He's one of the owners. The other guy is called George. Big guys, aren't they?"

"You're not kidding! Have you seen the muscles on him? Even his muscles have got muscles."

"Was he looking for me?"

"No. He just popped in to check what we did in here. He said that you'd told him you were a private investigator, but he seemed convinced we were a tanning salon."

Maybe I should change that sign after all.

"He also said that they were looking for a pretty young receptionist for their new venture."

"I hope you're not getting ideas again, Jules?"

"No. Of course not."

"Don't forget what happened last time you jumped

ship."

"It's all right, Jill. I'm here to stay this time. Besides which, I'm enjoying the knitting lessons from Mrs V, so I don't want to leave."

***

I'd asked Lacey Ball to come in and see me. She hadn't been very happy about it, but I'd explained that once I'd taken on a case, I couldn't drop it until the customer signed the 'case closure' form. She'd asked if I could post it to her, but I told her I had to witness her signature. All of that was of course complete nonsense. There was no such thing as a 'case closure' form. If someone wanted me to stop working on a case, all they had to do was stop paying me. The truth was, I wanted her to come to the office because I had a hunch, and I needed to test it out.

She arrived at eleven o'clock, as arranged. Jules showed her in, and offered her a drink, but Lacey seemed to be in a hurry, and declined.

"Do have a seat, Lacey."

"I don't know why I had to come in. I told you over the phone: I don't want to pursue this any longer. It was all a mistake. I don't know what I was thinking. I must have been dreaming or something. Mandy couldn't have called me. I saw her buried three years ago."

"If you can just sign this 'case closure' form, I'll work out your final bill, and that'll be the end of it."

"Okay."

I held out a sheet of paper and a pen. As she reached out to take them, I caught a glimpse of her hands. Yes! Just as I'd thought.

She was staring down at the paper. "There's nothing on here. It's a blank sheet of paper. I thought I had to sign a 'case closure' form?"

"Actually, that was a lie."

"What?"

"Sorry. There's no such thing as a 'case closure' form."

"Why did you get me in here, then?"

"I thought it was time that you and I had a heart to heart, *Mandy.*"

She looked shocked, and sat back in the chair. "What did you just call me?"

"Mandy. That *is* your name, isn't it?"

"I don't know what you're talking about."

"Why did you kill Lacey?"

"What do you mean? You're talking nonsense."

"You're not going to deny that you're Mandy, are you?"

She said nothing for several moments.

"Let me help you," I prompted. "My guess is that you and Joe fell in love. Is that right?"

She took a deep breath. "We didn't plan for it to happen. We spent a lot of time in each other's company, and just sort of fell for one another."

"What was Lacey's reaction?"

"She didn't know anything about it for a long time. Joe and I saw one another behind her back, but we knew we couldn't carry on like that forever. We decided that we had to tell her, and thought the kindest way to do it would be for both of us to talk to her together. We didn't want to hurt her, but we couldn't go on denying our love for one another. We knew she'd take it badly, but had no idea just *how* badly. She went hysterical. She flew into a rage, and started throwing things around the house. Then she stormed out, jumped into her car, and drove off at a ridiculous speed. I told Joe we had to follow her because I was afraid she'd hurt herself. We followed her in my car. It was night-time; there was nobody on the road. She was driving like a maniac. Then, when we got out into the countryside, she took a sharp bend way too fast, and the car left the road. The next thing I knew, there was a terrible impact. She'd hit a tree, and the car had burst into flames. We couldn't do anything. It was horrible. We couldn't get anywhere near it because of the heat."

"Why didn't you just call the police, and tell them what had happened?"

"I wanted to, but Joe said that it would all come out about us. People would blame us for Lacey's death. I didn't know what to do. I was in such a state. Joe said the best thing would be for us to pretend the person in the car was me. I could take over Lacey's life. He said that because we were identical twins, the DNA would match. All I had to do was throw some of my jewellery into the car."

"And since then, you've effectively lived your life as your sister?"

"Yes. We buried Lacey, and everyone thought it was me. Since then, Joe and I have lived together as man and wife."

"So what changed? Why did you come to see me, and make up a story about a phone call from your sister?"

"Joe and I were very much in love at first, but over the last few months, he's become more and more remote. Eventually, I found out why. He's been seeing another woman, much younger than me. I confronted him about it, but he didn't seem to care. He said he was going to leave me to go and live with her. I couldn't bear the thought of being alone, or that Lacey had died for nothing. If I didn't have Joe, then what was it all about?"

"I still don't understand why you came to see me."

"To scare Joe. I told him that if he left me, I'd tell the police what had happened, but he didn't believe me. He said, 'Go to the police if you like. You'll get arrested.' I knew he was right. The police wouldn't have believed me, and even if they had, I would have ended up in prison anyway. I thought that if Joe could see a private investigator was on the case, maybe that would scare him."

"I saw Joe talking to a young woman," I said. "I spoke to her after he'd gone. She said that he'd finished with her, but she had no idea why. She was expecting him to leave you and go live with her."

"He ended it because he knew it was the only way I'd tell you to drop the investigation. I still don't know how you knew I wasn't Lacey."

"There were a number of things. Everyone I talked to said that Lacey was into fashion, and took a lot of care over her appearance." I looked her up and down. "With respect, you don't fit that bill."

Mandy lowered her head. "I know. Lacey always dressed well."

"Also, just now when you took the paper from me, I noticed your fingernails."

Mandy glanced at them. "I've always bitten them. Lacey had beautiful nails. What's going to happen to me now?"

"I have to call the police."

"Must you? They'll throw me in prison."

"I have no choice. I don't know what will happen to

you, but if what you've told me about the crash is true, then even though you and Joe may have been the reason Lacey was driving recklessly, you didn't kill her. You didn't actually drive her off the road. You'll definitely be charged with something—maybe perverting the course of justice."

I called Leo Riley, who unsurprisingly wasn't very pleased to hear from me. But when I explained the circumstances, he sent a couple of uniformed officers to collect Mandy. She was a broken woman, and the truth was, I actually felt sorry for her.

***

A little later, I got a phone call from Kathy.

"You okay, Jill? You sound a bit down."

"Yeah, I'm okay. I've just closed a case, but it wasn't a particularly happy outcome."

"Do you want to talk about it?"

"Not really. It's fine."

"Okay. Well, look—the reason I called—it's about the housewarming. Pete wants to know whether you'd mind if he brought Jethro and Sebastian along with us? He mentioned the party to them, and they thought it might be fun."

"Haven't they got anything more exciting to do?"

"Apparently not."

Wow! That was pretty darn sad.

"Okay. I suppose so."

"Right. Well, we'll see you on Sunday. We're looking forward to it."

"Yeah. Me too." Not!

The house was going to be absolutely crammed. Still, having Sebastian and Jethro there could prove to be amusing when the twins spotted them.

When I got home, I was still reeling from the after-effects of the Lacey Ball affair. It was one of those times when I'd solved the case, but didn't feel good about it.

The house was looking really good, but not for long. It would be wrecked after the stupid housewarming party. Unless—

I'd just had a brilliant idea.

I had a little time before Jack came home, so I got together all of my furniture and shrank it. I then shrank some of Jack's furniture. It was then a trivial matter to swap the furniture before restoring it to full size. I put Jack's furniture in the living room and dining room, and mine out of harm's way in the spare bedroom. If anything was spilled now, it would be on Jack's horrible furniture, and not mine. After the housewarming was over, I could swap it back again.

I'd just finished when Jack came through the door. He looked rather confused.

"What's going on?"

"What do you mean?"

"When I went out this morning your furniture was in here, but now it's all mine."

"Oh that? Well, you did say that you wanted some of yours out, so I thought it only fair."

Chapter 21

The *big* day had arrived—the day of the housewarming party. This was all Jack's fault; him and his bright ideas. How was I ever going to get through the day? I hadn't been lying when I'd told Mrs Rollo that the catering was already in hand. As soon as I'd mentioned the party to Aunt Lucy, she'd insisted that she wanted to make all of the food, and I'd been more than happy to let her do it. She, Lester and the twins were going to bring it over later, so that was one problem I didn't have to worry about.

I felt a little happier about the house now that I'd hidden my furniture away. Snigger. Jack still hadn't worked out what I was up to, but he'd soon realise when it was transformed back again after the party was over. He'd had to go into work while I'd spent most of the morning tidying and cleaning. How long it would remain that way was anyone's guess. With the kids coming over, probably not long.

By four o'clock, the house was rammed full of people. They were in the living room, the dining room, the kitchen, and even in the hallway. I didn't know half of them, but then several were former colleagues of Jack's from Washbridge police station.

"Why did you let Mikey bring his drum?" I had collared Kathy.

"He wanted to show people how he's progressed."

"Don't you think there's enough noise in here without a drum?"

"That's why I said he could bring it—because I knew it was already going to be noisy."

I'd taken the kids upstairs to our bedroom. Although I was a little worried they might do some damage, it was better for them all to be together where they could play without being under our feet. I'd made sure they had plenty of cakes and pop. Even from downstairs, I could hear the thump, thump, thump of Mikey's drum. I felt sorry for the other kids.

"What's that?" Aunt Lucy said. She was standing next to the dining table, which was set out with all the food and nibbles that she'd prepared. She was looking at Mrs Rollo's cake. The so called Victoria sponge looked as though it had been thrown against a wall. It was flat on one side, and the middle had sunk.

"Err—it's a Victoria sponge," I said.

"You made a brave effort, Jill." Aunt Lucy gave me a sympathetic look. "It's a pity you dropped it."

"Actually, I made that," Mrs Rollo said.

I hadn't realised she was standing at the other end of the table. She was obviously very proud of her creation.

Aunt Lucy had a puzzled look on her face.

"Aunt Lucy, this is our neighbour, Mrs Rollo. She offered to do all the catering for us, but I told her that you already had it in hand. She insisted on making this Victoria sponge. It's very nice, isn't it?"

Aunt Lucy hesitated. "Err—it's—err—a very unusual shape."

"Delicious too." Mrs Rollo beamed. "Would you like to try a piece?"

"Perhaps later," Aunt Lucy said. "I think I can hear Lester calling me." And off she scuttled.

"What about you, Jill? Would you like a piece?"

"Maybe later. I've just had a rather large cupcake. I suppose I'd better mingle, and check everyone is okay."

Jules was sitting on a stool at the breakfast bar. Next to her was a young man who I realised must be Gilbert. His face was covered in spots, and he was in the process of squeezing the one on his nose. I approached them from the rear just to be safe.

"Hi, Jules."

"Oh, hi, Jill. This party is really good. Thanks for inviting us. This is Gilbert."

When he turned around to face me, he was still squeezing his spot.

"Hello, Gilbert."

"Thank you for inviting me."

"No problem. Help yourself to drinks and nibbles." With that, I moved out of the line of fire.

Wow. Jules must really like that guy to stick with him.

"What on earth is going on, Jill?" Kathy said. She grabbed me by the arm, and frogmarched me into the hallway.

"What do you mean?"

"Who's that woman who has Pete cornered in the living room?"

I looked through the open door. Megan Lovemore was standing in front of Peter, who was backed up against the wall. He looked terrified.

"That's Megan."

"Who on earth is Megan, and why is she monopolising my husband?"

"She's our next door neighbour. Her husband died in

tragic circumstances a few years ago."

"That's very sad, but she'll be the one dying in tragic circumstances if she gets any closer to Pete."

"It's okay, Kathy. Megan wants to start her own gardening business, and I happened to mention that Peter—"

"I might have known you'd be behind this."

"Hold on. I only said that Peter was a professional gardener, and might be able to give her some tips."

"I'll give her some tips if she gets any closer to my husband."

With that, Kathy stormed off towards Peter and Megan.

"We've got a bone to pick with you." Pearl tapped me on the shoulder.

"Yes, we have," Amber said.

Oh boy! What now?

"What's the matter, girls? Aren't you enjoying the party?"

"The party is great," Amber said. "And the food is lovely, but then Mum's food is always lovely."

"The Victoria sponge is a bit of a mess though," Pearl said. "But never mind the food. Why didn't you tell us?"

"You're going to have to give me a bit more than that."

"About Jethro?" Pearl said.

"And Sebastian," Amber added.

"Oh yeah. Jethro and Sebastian. Didn't I mention that they'd be here?"

"You know you didn't," Amber said. "How come they are?"

"They both work for Peter. He has his own gardening business now."

"How long have they been working for him?"

"Jethro has been with him for just over a year. Sebastian has only recently joined him."

"And you conveniently forgot to tell us?"

"Why would I tell you?"

"Because they're the hottest guys in Candlefield, so we have a right to know."

"Isn't there something you're forgetting?"

"What's that?" Amber huffed.

"The small matter that you're both married now."

"That doesn't stop us looking, does it? If you'd told us they were in Washbridge, we'd probably have come over sooner."

"Well, you're here now, but if you insist on ogling them, please don't let Alan and William catch you."

"We've never *ogled* anyone." Amber looked put out.

"The very thought of it," Pearl said.

I hadn't seen much of Jack. He'd been with his buddies from Washbridge police station for most of the evening. Every time I'd walked past them, they'd been talking about bowling. It was amazing how boring men could be.

"How's it going, petal?" Jack tapped me on the shoulder.

"Nice of you to find time for me. And don't call me petal."

"I've been circulating with our friends."

"No, you haven't. You've been stuck in that corner with your buddies talking about bowling for the last two hours."

"You're exaggerating again."

"Anyway, everything seems to be going okay."

"Yeah, I think so." He glanced at the table. "What on earth is wrong with that sponge cake?"

"Mrs Rollo made it."

"Can't you throw it in the bin or something?"

"How can I? She's hovering around the table, waiting for people to take a piece. I can hardly pick it up and dump it in the bin in front of her, can I?"

"I suppose not. I see Megan's got Peter cornered." Jack laughed.

"Yeah. Kathy just gave me a right ear bashing. She's not impressed at all."

"I don't imagine she is."

Just then, someone thumped on the front door.

"Who's that?" Jack said.

"How should I know? I can't see through wood. I thought everyone was here."

"Maybe it's the neighbours from down the road, come to complain about the noise."

When I opened the door, there stood Norman Hosey.

"Hello, you two. I couldn't help but notice you're having some sort of party. Housewarming, is it?"

"Yeah."

"I do love housewarming parties. My invitation must have gone astray. Anyway, I'm here now." He walked straight past us, and made a beeline for the food and drink.

"I pity the poor soul who ends up standing next to him," Jack said.

"Yeah. Maybe we should introduce him to Kathy."

"You are horrible to your sister." He laughed. "Anyway, I'm glad your birth family could make it. It's nice to see them at long last. Your aunt Lucy is lovely, and the food she made is fantastic."

"I'll tell her you said that. She'll be pleased."

"And the twins, they're very bubbly, aren't they?"

"That's one word for it. They've got their eyes on Peter's employees."

"Really? But aren't the twins married?"

"Yeah. Even so, I think we'd better warn Jethro and Sebastian."

After Jack had disappeared again, I bumped into Blake.

"Hi, Jill. Thanks for inviting us. This is Jen, my wife."

Jen was petite and really pretty; she had a lovely smile.

"Nice to meet you, Jill," she said. "We're really pleased that you've moved in across the road from us. There aren't many couples our age around here. Maybe the four of us could have dinner some time?"

"That would be nice. We'd love to."

"And, maybe you and I could have a girls' night out, or go shopping somewhere together? I used to live in London, but I moved up here to do a course. That's when I met Blake. I don't really have many friends up here."

"That would be great. I'll look forward to it."

I carried on mingling. Jen seemed really nice, and I hoped we could become friends, but it might prove difficult. It was a strange position to be in. I knew more about her husband than she did. That could make our friendship very awkward.

I needed a breather, so I went upstairs to the back bedroom to get away from all the noise. When I tried to open the door, it seemed to catch on something. Or someone.

"Do you mind?" A voice came from inside.

"Grandma?"

"Stop bashing the door against my arm."

I managed to squeeze inside. Grandma and Mrs V were sitting on two of my chairs. On the floor between them were two wine bottles. One of them was empty.

"What are you two doing in here? Didn't Armi come with you, Mrs V?"

"He couldn't make it. He had a prior engagement at the Cuckoo Clock Appreciation Society."

"It's far too noisy downstairs." Grandma complained. "All that jibber-jabber. I can't hear myself think. Annabel and I decided to come up here to get a bit of peace and quiet."

"Isn't the drum annoying you?"

"It was. Until I dealt with it."

"You've helped yourselves to wine, I see."

"Just a glass or two." Grandma hiccupped. Mrs V's eyes looked a little glazed.

"Are you okay, Mrs V?"

"Oh yes, Jill. I'm having a wonderful time. Your grandmother is great company. We always have fun when we're out together."

"I can remember the last time you two had a night out. I seem to remember boomerangs and boxer shorts were involved."

"I don't know what you're talking about," Grandma said. "I remember no such thing. Now, if you wouldn't mind, Annabel and I were having an interesting conversation. Why don't you go downstairs and attend to your guests?"

"Okay. Just don't overdo it with the wine."

The party finally broke up at half past midnight. Most of the guests had ordered taxis, including Mrs V who was a little bit the worse for wear. The twins, Grandma, Aunt Lucy, and Lester all made out that they'd parked down the road, and set out on foot. I knew full well that as soon as they were out of sight, they'd magic themselves back to Candlefield.

When the house was finally empty, I took a look around. It was a scene of devastation. Fortunately, it didn't look as though anyone had spilled anything on the carpets, but there were glasses, plates, and spent party poppers everywhere. The table was covered with leftovers. It was a dreadful mess.

"Let's leave this until the morning," Jack said.

"Are you kidding? I can't wake up to this mess."

"But I just want to go to bed. I'm tired."

"Drunk more like."

"I am *not* drunk."

"How much did you have to drink?"

"I don't know. Not much."

"You go up. I'll be up in a little while."

I poured myself a small glass of wine. I deliberately hadn't drunk much during the evening because I'd wanted to keep my wits about me.

After about thirty minutes, I heard the sound of snoring. That was my cue. I used every magic spell in the book, and within half an hour, the place was spick and span. Now I could go to bed. Now I could relax. I was never going to move house again, not if it meant having another housewarming party.

Chapter 22

Mrs V was nowhere to be seen when I arrived for work the next morning. That was hardly surprising after she'd spent most of the evening with Grandma. I could have called Jules to ask her to come in on her day off, but I figured it wasn't going to be all that busy.

Winky was on my desk, looking just like a parent waiting for their teenager to come home after a night out.

"I hope you have a good excuse!" he said, as soon as I walked through the door.

"For what?"

"You know what."

"I have no idea what you are talking about."

"Why wasn't I invited to your housewarming party?"

Oh bum. "What housewarming party?"

"The one you had yesterday."

"Oh, that one. I wish I could have invited you, but like I said before, we're not allowed to have any animals in the house."

"You invited the old bag lady who is about as much use as a chocolate fireguard. And you invited Jules, who although very pretty, has only worked for you for five minutes. But you failed to invite the most important member of your team!"

"Who would that be?"

If looks could kill, I would have been an ex-P.I.

"*That* would be me."

"Look, I'm really sorry, Winky. You didn't miss anything. It was pretty rubbish."

"All the more reason to have invited me. I would have really got the party started."

"I've brought you some cake."

"Really?" His face lit up.

"Of course. You didn't think I'd forgotten you, did you?"

"Where is it?"

I took the box out of my bag. "Here you are. I'll put it in your bowl. You do like Victoria sponge, don't you?"

Because I had no PA/receptionist, I had to man the phone myself.

"Jill Gooder. How can I help you?"

"I'd like to book a stand-up tanning session, please. Do you have any slots free this afternoon?"

"We don't do tanning."

"Oh? I saw the orange sign and thought —"

"Sorry. No tanning here. Bye."

I really was going to have to change that sign, or perhaps I should just move into the tanning business. I certainly got more inquiries for tanning than I ever did as a private investigator.

I grabbed what was left of the Yellow Pages, and found the section for signage. The most eye-catching ad was for a company in Washbridge called 'It's A Sign'. I gave them a call.

"Hello, It's A Sign." A sing-song voice answered.

"I need a new sign for my business."

"That's what we do!" The sing-song voice was getting to me a bit, but I persevered.

"Would it be possible to have someone come out and give me a price for a new sign?"

"Of course!"

"How soon could you send someone?"

"Where are you located?"

I gave him the office address.

"As luck would have it, I have another job in that area. I can come around later today, if that suits?"

"That would be great. See you later."

By the time I'd finished on the call, I'd more or less lost the will to live. Why couldn't he speak normally? Still, hopefully it would be worth it. I needed a sign that conveyed the right message. One which let people know I was a P.I, and not some silly tanning salon.

There was nothing much happening in the office — even Winky was asleep, so I magicked myself over to Cuppy C.

"Did you enjoy yourselves yesterday, girls?"

Amber and Pearl were both behind the counter in the tea room.

"Yes, thanks, Jill. I really enjoyed it," Amber said.

"Yeah, me too." Pearl nodded. "Mind you, the guys aren't speaking to us again."

"You're always falling out. What have you done this time?"

"They reckon we spent too much time talking to Jethro and Sebastian."

"You did seem to spend a lot of time with them."

"We were only asking how they were getting on in their new jobs. That was all. We were just being friendly."

"You weren't flirting with them, then?"

"No," Amber said. "Of course not! We're married women now."

"How's the P.I. business?" Pearl asked. "Anything exciting happening?"

"Not really. It's pretty quiet at the moment. The most

exciting thing I've done today was ring someone about my sign."

"I thought you'd only just got a new one? Has it broken already?"

"No, but it's obviously conveying the wrong message. I keep getting phone calls from people wanting to book a sunbed, so I'm going to get someone to design me a completely new sign. Something that says: 'Private Investigator'."

"Actually," Pearl said. "That's not a bad idea. We might not be able to change the name of Cuppy C, but we could change our sign."

Amber's eyes lit up. "That's a great idea. We've had that sign ever since we opened. It's a bit boring—a bit plain. We could get something really exciting which would put Best Cakes to shame."

"Are you sure about this, girls? Everyone loves Cuppy C just as it is, and that includes the sign."

"Dead sure! It'll be brilliant!" Pearl was way too excited by the idea. We'll still have all of our regular customers, but the new sign will attract new ones. We'll have to get somebody in, Amber."

"Yeah. What should we have on the sign?"

That was my cue to leave. I left the girls discussing their new signage, and went upstairs; Flora and Laura were up there, chatting. I wasn't sure what sort of reception I'd get because we hadn't got off to a very good start.

"Hi, Jill," Flora called.

I didn't want to be mean-spirited, so I said, "Hi."

"Jill, could we have a word with you, please?" Laura stepped forward.

What was this all about? What did they have planned

now? The doors to their rooms were open, and I could see they were both neat and tidy; a total contrast to the last time I'd been there.

"Look, Jill," Flora said. "We'd like to apologise."

"Oh?"

"Yeah," Laura nodded. "We were totally out of order. We were so excited at getting these rooms that we had a few too many drinks, and then, well, we kind of lost our heads. I know we were rude to you, so we just wanted to say we're sorry. It won't happen again."

"Okay then, but if it does, I'll have to tell the twins."

"We promise. You won't have any more problems with us." Laura drew a finger across her heart.

For some reason, I still didn't trust them. Maybe it was because I'd seen them with Miles Best. I couldn't help but think they were up to something, and that their 'butter wouldn't melt' act was all part of some sinister plan.

When I went back downstairs, Daze was sitting in the corner.

"Hi, Daze. How's things?"

"Remarkably quiet, but I'm not complaining. I'm ready for a bit of a break."

"Daze, can I ask you something?"

"Sure, fire away."

"I've already mentioned this to Grandma. I haven't seen Ma Chivers or Alicia for over a year now. According to Grandma, a lot of the wicked witches have disappeared from Candlefield for no apparent reason. You wouldn't know anything about it, would you?"

She beckoned me to sit down. "I don't want what I'm about to tell you to go beyond these walls."

"Okay."

"Something's afoot, but I don't know what. It isn't just the wicked witches who have gone AWOL. A lot of other criminals—all sup types: vampires, werewolves, witches, wizards—you name it—all seem to have gone to ground. No one knows where they've gone or what they're up to. If they'd all moved to the human world, we'd have heard about it by now, but there's been nothing."

"That's interesting, and a little scary."

"You're right there. I can't help but feel that something big is about to happen. I just hope I'm wrong."

***

A few hours later, back at the office, a man popped his head around the door.

"Hello there. I'm from It's A Sign, I believe you're expecting me?" the man said in the same sing-song voice I'd heard on the phone.

"Yes, thanks for coming in so quickly. Mr—?"

"Song, Sid Song."

He said everything in a sing-song fashion, and I was having difficulty concentrating. I felt like I needed to reply in song, but resisted the urge. Instead, I took him through to my office.

"So, Mr Song, is that why you speak like that? Is it a gimmick?"

He looked puzzled. "Speak like what?" he said, in his sing-song way.

"Like—never mind."

"It was quite fortunate that you called when you did," he sang.

"Oh? Why's that?"

"I already had an appointment in this very building. In fact, I've just this minute finished with the two gentlemen next door."

"You mean the new health club?"

"That's right. So, Miss Gooder, what exactly is it you're looking for?"

"I don't know if you saw it when you came in, but I already have a sign outside."

"I didn't notice it. I did see the one for the tanning salon though."

"That's actually my sign."

"I thought you were a private investigator."

"I am. Never mind. Look, I need a sign that says: *Jill Gooder, Private Investigator*. I don't want it to say P.I. because you'd be surprised how many people don't know what that stands for."

"Would you like anything else on the sign? Maybe a magnifying glass or a cat?"

"Why would I want a cat on it?"

"You've got a cat there in the window. I thought perhaps he was part of the team."

"Definitely no cats or magnifying glasses. Just the words, '*Jill Gooder, Private Investigator*'."

"Right you are."

"And this is the important part. The colours—I don't want anyone thinking it's a tanning salon or a nail bar."

"So, probably blue on white, or black on white?"

"I'll leave that to you, Mr Song. As long as I end up with something that says I'm a serious private investigator."

"Okay, I'll go and take some measurements, and I'll give you a call later today."

"Excellent."

As soon as he'd left, Winky jumped onto my desk.

"Why was that guy singing all the time?"

"I don't know."

"You have a bad habit of attracting all the nutjobs."

Wasn't that the truth?

***

There was no sign of Mr Ivers on the toll bridge, which was something of a relief. When I arrived home, Mrs Rollo was in the garden again.

"Hello, Jill. Thank you for inviting me to your housewarming. I really enjoyed it."

"No problem. Thank you for the cake."

"I noticed there was quite a bit left when I went home."

"Don't worry about that. I took it to the office with me today, and it's all been eaten now."

"Has it?" She beamed. "That's good to know. I hate to see waste."

"Me, too."

Once inside the house, I set about reversing the sequence of spells that I'd cast before the party. I took all of Jack's furniture back up to the spare bedroom, and got all of mine out. Minutes later, my furniture was back where it should be, without a blemish on it. That had been a great idea of mine.

Just then, there was a knock at the door. It was Megan.

"I hope you don't mind me calling around like this."

"Not at all. Aren't you working today?"

"No. I don't have any bookings, so I'm starting to put together my business plan. Your brother-in-law, Peter, was very helpful."

"So I noticed."

"He gave me lots of good advice. The problem was, he gave me so much, I can't remember everything he said. I was just wondering if there was some way I could meet up with him. I could take a notepad with me this time, and make some proper notes. Do you think that might be possible?"

"I can certainly ask him."

"Would you, Jill? That's really kind of you."

"No problem. Leave it with me. I'll have a word with Peter, and see what he says. I'll let you know as soon as I can."

"Thanks, Jill. You're a good friend."

After Megan had gone, I called Kathy. This should be interesting. Snigger.

"Kathy?"

"Hi. Have you got your place straightened up after the party?"

"Yeah. Just about. Did you, Peter and the kids enjoy it?"

"The kids had a great time. They've made some new friends. Pete *certainly* had a great time with your bimbo of a neighbour."

"Bimbo?"

"You know who I mean. He was talking to her for most of the night. You're going to have to watch that one with Jack."

"I don't have to worry about that. Jack only has eyes for me."

"Yeah, well, just watch her."

"It's funny you should mention Megan."

"Why?"

"She's just been over here to see me. She said how helpful Peter had been."

"Yeah. I bet she did."

"No, honestly. She was really pleased that he'd helped her with her plans for her gardening business."

"Hmm."

"Anyway, she wondered if they could meet up to go over it in more detail, so she could make some notes."

"Are you serious?"

"She only wants to talk to him, Kathy."

"Yeah? Well, she can whistle."

"What shall I say when she asks?"

"Do you really want me to tell you?"

"Probably not."

Chapter 23

Jack didn't get in until long after I'd gone to bed, so I wasn't able to tell him about Megan until the next morning.

"Your favourite neighbour came to see me last night."

"Mr Hosey?"

"Very funny. Megan came around."

"What did she want?"

"To say thanks for the party, and for all the help that Peter gave her with putting together a business plan."

"So *that's* what the two of them were doing, is it?" He grinned.

"She wants Peter to meet up with her again because she wasn't able to remember everything he said."

"I wonder what Kathy will have to say about that." He laughed.

"I've already spoken to her. She's not very thrilled about the idea. I don't know what I'm going to tell Megan. And, that's not all Kathy said. She reckons I'd better watch you with Megan because she'll be after you next."

"You're not jealous, are you, Jill?"

"Of Megan? Of course I'm not. You wouldn't dare wander."

"Wouldn't dare?"

"That's right. You know what the consequences would be if you did."

"Would I enjoy them?"

"Possibly."

"Anyway, I've got to get going. Don't forget, I'm working late tonight."

"Until what time?"

"I don't know. The boss said we might be there until midnight, so expect me when you see me."

"I thought the idea of us moving in together was to spend more time in each other's company?"

"We do."

"Not as much as you spend with the stupid police force."

"Come on, Jill. You know what the job's like. It's the same when you're working a case."

"I know. I'm only kidding. Come here and give me a kiss."

***

I set off about thirty minutes after Jack had left. I'd just turned the corner at the end of the street when I noticed a familiar figure standing at the bus stop. It was Jen. I pulled up alongside her, and wound the window down.

"Jen! Are you going into Washbridge?"

"Yeah, I'm waiting for the number seventeen."

"Jump in, I'll give you a lift."

"Thanks." She climbed in beside me.

"Do you catch the bus every day?"

"No, my car's gone in for a service. Blake's gone away for a couple of days, for work, so he couldn't give me a lift. I'm glad you pulled up. I didn't even know what the fare was. Oh, and thanks for inviting us to the housewarming. We had a really good time."

"Me too," I lied.

"We were surprised you'd invited Mr Hosey."

"We didn't; he invited himself."

"That explains it." She laughed. "Has he tried to sign

you up for the neighbourhood watch?"

"Yeah, we'd only been in the house ten minutes before he asked us to join."

"Whatever you do, don't ask to see his train set."

"Don't worry, I don't intend to."

"Don't even hint that you might be interested in trains. Blake made the mistake of saying he enjoyed the occasional train journey, and the next thing we knew, we'd been invited to Mr Hosey's place. We were there for three hours. He told us about every single train. I was nearly comatose by the time we escaped. It was awful."

Talking of boring people, we were just approaching the toll bridge. Much to my relief, it wasn't Mr Ivers in the booth.

"What's happened to the new man?" I asked the skinny, ginger haired man who took my forty pence.

"Do you mean the movie nut?"

"Yeah, I guess I do."

"He was useless. He spent all his time trying to persuade people to sign up for some stupid newsletter he writes. As if anyone would be that crazy."

As if. "Did he get sacked?"

"Nah. They've transferred him to an office job."

"Does that mean he won't be working on the bridge again?"

"No. You won't be seeing him again."

"Yes!" I shouted, and gave a fist pump.

Jen gave me a puzzled look.

***

When I arrived at the office building, I was delighted to

see that my new sign had been installed. Despite his stupid singing habit, Sid Song had come through. He'd given me a good price, and had been able to complete the job in record time. He'd said something about being able to give me a good deal because he was doing a similar job in the area. Whatever the reason, I couldn't have been happier. The new sign was just what I'd asked for, and was in a font and colour that would leave no one in any doubt that mine was a serious business.

Jill Gooder
Private Investigator

Sid Song's van was still parked outside the building, but there was no sign of him. Maybe he was in my office waiting to be paid.

Jules was behind the desk; she was knitting.

"It looks like you've caught the bug."

"I love it, Jill. I never thought I'd enjoy knitting, but it's really good fun. Look at this."

"What is it, exactly, Jules?"

"A scarf."

"Oh yeah. Is it meant to be wider in some places than others?"

"I don't know why it's gone like that. Do you have any idea?"

"No, sorry. It's an interesting design though. Has the sign man been in?"

"Yes. He left you this." She handed me an invoice.

"Where is he now?"

"He just dropped the invoice off, and then left." She shrugged. "Oh, by the way, Jill, I've dumped Gilbert."

"Really? After you brought him to the party?"

"That's what made my mind up. He was squeezing his spots all night. It was embarrassing. I didn't know where to put myself. So anyway, I'm young, free and single again now."

"Good for you."

"Who were those two gorgeous guys at the party?"

"You don't mean William and Alan, the twins' husbands, do you?"

"No. The really buff guys. I think they came with your brother-in-law."

"Oh, you mean Jethro and Sebastian."

"Nice names. Do you know them well?"

"Not well. They used to work for my aunt Lucy as gardeners, and now they work for Peter."

"Do you know if they have girlfriends?"

"I honestly don't know, Jules, but I can ask Peter if you'd like me to."

"Would you, please?"

"Yeah, of course. I'll find out for you."

***

I was more nervous than I'd been for a long time. It was almost exactly a year since I'd started teaching my class of new wizards and witches. At the beginning, I'd been really nervous. Grandma had dropped me in it, and I hadn't been sure how I'd cope. For a while, I'd found it very difficult, but the longer it had gone on, the more I'd got into it, and the more confident I'd become.

The kids had been really great; they were all so enthusiastic. I loved to see their faces when they came across a spell for the first time. To be involved with magic at that age was fantastic, and once again I realised what I'd missed out on as a child. Most of the kids had taken to it like a duck to water. I barely needed to coach them at all. But two or three of them had struggled, and found it much more difficult. It was those kids that I'd spent the most time with. I'd even given some of them one-to-one tuition.

Today was the culmination of the year's teaching. Today they were all to take their level one test. I'd never had to go through this because my move up the levels had been very informal. Grandma had been my teacher. She'd been the one who decided when I could move to the next level, but for most kids in Candlefield there was a proper procedure. They studied a level for a year, and then at the end of that year they sat their level test. If they passed, they moved up to the next level. If they didn't, they stayed behind, and had to study the same level for another year.

The twins had never progressed beyond level two, something which apparently wasn't uncommon. According to what I've been told, the average pass rate from beginner to level one was about eighty percent, which was fairly high. There was a much lower pass rate from level one to two, and it got progressively lower as you went up the levels. I couldn't bear the thought that any of my kids might fail, but it was out of my hands now. Although I had to be there, I wasn't allowed to help them. I just had to sit and watch. It was going to be one of the hardest things I'd ever done.

At least I got to talk to them before the test started.

"Okay, you lot. Gather around. How are you all feeling?"

"Really scared, Miss," Tim said.

"There's nothing to be afraid of."

"I'm excited," Celine said. She was probably the most naturally gifted witch in the class.

"As long as you do your best, that's all that matters. Some of you may not pass. It's okay as long as you've tried your best. There's no shame in having to take level one for more than one year. Some people go up the levels quickly. Others take longer. It's all good."

"Miss Gooder." A voice came from my right. It was an elderly woman with a very serious expression. "It's time for the test to begin. I'm sorry, but you'll have to leave your class now. You can go and sit over there with the others."

I joined the four other teachers who were also waiting for their classes to take the level one test.

"Nerve-racking isn't it?" The young woman next to me said.

"You're not kidding. Have you done this before?"

"Oh, yes. I've taken level one students for the last seven years."

"Does it get any easier?"

"No. If anything it gets worse. Last year, only seventy-seven percent of mine got through. I felt like I'd let them down, but they always bounce back because they're very resilient."

"I have no idea how mine are going to do."

"I'm sure if you've taught them, Jill, they'll be fine."

The test lasted just under an hour. The examiner chose a number of spells at random, and had each of the kids perform them. They were judged on how quickly the spell was cast, how effective the spell was, and also how well they coped when something went wrong. Did they recover quickly, or did they panic?

When it was over, the kids were sent to play in the far corner of the Range while the examiners conferred and marked the tests. An hour later, the kids were called back. By then I was a complete nervous wreck. The examiner called each of the kids up to the front by their name, in alphabetical order. I'd expected them to say out loud whether each child had passed or failed, but instead the kids were handed a slip of paper. Even so, it was easy to tell the result by looking at the child's face when they came away. Some beamed with delight—others were in tears.

I watched as each of my students' names was called: A smile, another smile, another smile. All passes so far.

There were only three of them left. So far everyone had passed. Now it was Tim's turn. I was more worried about him than any of the others. He was obviously hesitant as he looked at his result, but then his face lit up, and he came rushing over.

"I passed, Miss! I passed! I'm level one!"

The last two were the same. Every one of my kids had passed. They were now all on level one. I was so excited for them.

"Miss!" Celine said. "We've got something for you. We put our pocket money together and bought you these." She passed me a small, gift-wrapped package. I opened it to find a box of chocolates.

"We asked your cousins if we should get you flowers or chocolates. They said you'd rather have chocolates. We just wanted to say thank you for teaching us."

I was so choked I could barely speak. A tear trickled

down my cheek.

"Thank you."

After all the kids had gone, and the Range was almost empty, I found the head teacher who looked after all the teaching staff.

"Well done, Jill," she said.

"Thanks, Miranda. I'm so delighted for the kids."

"You've done an excellent job. It's the best result we've ever had."

"Thanks, but that's not really down to me. That's down to the children themselves. Look, Miranda, there's something I need to talk to you about."

"What's that?"

"I'm going to have to drop my teaching duties."

"You can't do that. Look how well you've done."

"I know, but I've recently moved into a new house in the human world, and even though time stands still when I'm over here, I find the effort of teaching drains me. Also, I'm getting more and more demands on my time here in Candlefield. Then of course, I have my own business in the human world."

"What are you saying? Don't you want to teach ever again?"

"I need a break for at least a year. Then I'll review it again. I wouldn't want to do it unless I'm able to put my whole heart and soul into it."

"Okay, Jill. I understand. Thank you for everything you've done this year."

"It's been my absolute pleasure."

***

I caught up with Tabitha Hathaway at the offices of the Combined Sup Council.

"Jill, nice to see you again. I assume you've come to a decision?"

"If the offer's still open, I'd very much like to join the board of the Combined Sup Council."

"That's excellent news, I'm delighted. When will you be able to take up your post?"

"Pretty much immediately. When's the next meeting?"

"In a week's time. If you give me your number, I'll send you a text with all the details: time, place, that sort of thing. I'll be able to introduce you to the rest of the council at the meeting."

"That's fine, I'm looking forward to it."

I still wasn't sure if I'd made the right decision, but Grandma was right. I had to put my new powers to good use. I owed it to the Candlefield community to use those powers for good. And what better way to do that than to represent the witches on the Combined Sup Council? Now that I'd given up teaching for a year, I figured I'd be able to serve at least twelve months on the council. That should be enough time to see whether I could make a contribution or not. Of course, the real reason I'd agreed was that I was scared to tell Grandma I'd said no.

***

It was late afternoon, and I was amusing myself by flicking paperclips at Winky.

What? I didn't actually hit him. Sheesh, can't a girl have any fun?

Kathy arrived unannounced; she was crying with laughter.

"Are you all right?"

"Yeah, I'll be okay in a minute." She wiped the tears from her eyes. "Just give me a moment to recover." She grabbed a seat.

"What on earth is tickling you?"

"Jill, you are an absolute star. I don't know how you manage it."

"I have no idea what you're talking about. Have you been at the bottle again?"

"No, I haven't. It's that new sign of yours."

"My sign? What's funny about it?"

"It's brilliant. I haven't laughed so much in ages."

I had no idea what she was talking about—it had looked fine to me. Was there a spelling error that I'd missed? It was easy to see what you expected to see. Don't tell me they'd misspelled my name, and I hadn't realised it.

"Stay here." I dashed out of the office, down the stairs and across the road to get a better view.

"What the—?"

When I'd seen the sign earlier, mine was the only one on the building. Since then Sid had installed another immediately below mine. The second sign was in exactly the same font and colours, and read: 'I-Sweat'.

The two signs were so similar, and so close together that they gave the impression of a single sign that read:

Jill Gooder
Private Investigator
I-Sweat

Sid had never mentioned that he intended to give me a sign in the same font and colours as the I-Sweat guys. What had he been thinking? He probably hadn't been thinking—he'd been too busy singing.

I hurried back to the office.

"You can stop laughing, Kathy. It's not funny."

"Oh, come on, Jill. You have to see the funny side. *Jill Gooder - Private Investigator - I Sweat.*"

Out of the corner of my eye, I could see Winky rolling around the floor in hysterics.

"Why did you put 'I-Sweat' on the sign?" Kathy spluttered.

"I didn't. The 'I-Sweat' bit doesn't belong to me. That's the name of the new business which is moving in next door. It's a gym or a health club or something."

"Not a tanning salon, then?"

"I'm not in the mood. I've had it up to here with signs. I should have just left my dad's old one up."

"What are you going to do about it?"

"Kill somebody. And sing while I do it."

"You should be grateful to whoever fitted the sign."

"Grateful? Why would I be grateful?"

"I actually came here to pick a bone with you, but after I'd seen the sign, I couldn't hold it together."

"What have I done now?"

"Guess who rang Pete last night?"

"Santa Claus. I don't know. Who?"

"Your bimbo of a next door neighbour."

"Megan?"

"None other. Did you give her Pete's number?"

"No, I didn't."

"Are you sure."

"I'm positive."

"What about Jack?"

"I don't know. I suppose he could have."

"Well, you can tell Jack that when I see him again, he and I are going to have words."

"So, is Peter going to see Megan?"

"Oh, yes. He's only gone and invited her over to our house, so they can go through her business plan together."

"That will be cosy." I couldn't hold back a smirk.

"You can wipe that stupid smile off your face."

***

When Jen came around at seven o'clock, she had two huge cupcakes with her.

"I thought we could have these with a drink."

"Thanks." I took them from her. "I'd bought some custard creams, but these look lovely."

"I don't actually like custard creams. I think they're horrible."

What? It was a good thing she hadn't told me that before I'd asked her over. What kind of person didn't like custard creams? Still, the cupcakes did look lovely.

It turned out that she was a nurse, based in Washbridge Hospital.

"That must be very satisfying work."

"It is. Probably not as interesting as what you do though. If it hadn't been for my job, I would never have met Blake. I came up here to do a nursing course, and that's when we met. I transferred up here to finish my studies at Washbridge Hospital, and I've been there ever since."

"Do you see yourself staying in Washbridge, and in that job?"

"For the time being, yeah. Although Blake and I would like to have children some time. Not for a few years yet though." She hesitated.

"What's the matter, Jen?"

"It's nothing, it's just that—I don't know. Perhaps everyone feels this way."

"What way?"

"I know Blake loves me, but ever since we've been together, I've felt like he doesn't open up to me completely. It's like there's a part of his life that I don't even know about. Do you know what I mean?"

"Oh yeah, I know exactly what you mean."

ALSO BY ADELE ABBOTT

The Witch P.I. Mysteries:

The Susan Hall Mysteries:

Whoops! Our New Flatmate Is A Human.
Whoops! All The Money Went Missing.
Whoops! There's A Canary In My Coffee
See web site for availability.

AUTHOR'S WEB SITE
http:www.AdeleAbbott.com

FACEBOOK
http://www.facebook.com/AdeleAbbottAuthor

MAILING LIST
(new release notifications only)
http:/AdeleAbbott.com/adele/new-releases/

18260922R00121

Printed in Great Britain
by Amazon